1990

1990

SATISH GARIBAH

REACH PUBLISHERS

ISBN 978-1-77636-797-9

Published by Satish Garibah using Reach Publishers' services,
P O Box 1384, Wandsbeck, South Africa, 3631

Edited by Vanessa Finaughty for Reach Publishers
Cover designed by Reach Publishers
Website: www.reachpublishers.org
E-mail: reach@reachpublishers.org

SATISH GARIBAH

satishgaribahwriter@gmail.com

Table of Contents

CHAPTER ONE

The Love

It is 1990. The '80s have just ended and the new decade is about to bring new possibilities and new hope, something I am hoping will happen tonight. This is where my story begins. I remember ringing the doorbell. I remember its tone; it always sounds like I am ringing the door to Heaven. There is this divine melody to that ringing sound. I stand there staring at the door. The oak finish on the door is beautiful and majestic. Oh… yeah… I am still standing here, staring at this door. My palms are beginning to sweat just a bit, but it's cold out, so… Why am I sweating? My heart's beginning to race; it's like those moments when you watch your favourite soccer team almost score a goal, the adrenaline and rush, the nervousness and hype. I can feel the thud through my shirt; my heart is beating faster. I continue to stare at the door. The sound of the doorbell has long since died down; the silence in the air is deafening. The door handle begins to twitch. My heart is now racing even faster and the door begins to slowly open. Holy crap! Why does it feel like time is slowing? I understand the theory of relativity, but it is completely ridiculous how slow my perspective of time is at this moment. This moment… well, at this moment, all I can do is wipe my hands on the side of this very nice suit. The door is still swinging open. Hey… What are you going to say? *Hi, Mr Singh, I am A-Jay.* A-Jay? That is so dumb; your parents didn't take the time to name you Ajay so you can call yourself A-Jay. Wait a minute. I already met her dad before. The door now opens a little more. I can see a hand near the door handle. Man does Mr Singh have such a small wrist! That can't be right… Small wrist? Why is this door taking so long to open? This is insanity; no way can time move so slowly. It seems as if it's been five minutes since the door handle first moved.

The door swings open. Finally. It feels almost like I spent an entire lifetime waiting. Time seems to stand still as I just stare at Ria as if it is the first time I am laying my eyes on her. It is like looking at an angel staring at me from the gates of Heaven. There she stands: Ria Singh. How do I describe her? She is perfect. Right, that does not really describe her to you, now does it? But, to me, that is what she is: perfect. We have been friends since primary school. We walked to and from school together every day since then and we went to the same high school and the same college and, somewhere through all those days, I started seeing her very differently. Mind you, we have never actually dated until tonight. We actually never dated anyone else either. I never understood why she didn't; it isn't as if most guys had never looked at her that way…. Right, back to where I am. Ria Singh. She is about five-foot-four – just for the record, so am I. Definitely no hero type like in the movies. I am just the average joker in most of those Bollywood movies. You know the comedic relief sidekick to the hero; that's me. Haha… Dummy. Moving on. She has long dark brown hair that is just below her shoulders, and a fair complexion, like that matters much, because it is her personality that is as bright as the sun. She has piercing hazel eyes, the type of eyes that pierce through your soul when she looks at you, and a smile that can shift the energy in a room in a fraction of a second. She is the life of the party… no, she *is* the party. Every moment with her alters time itself. I mean, come on. It takes that door a lifetime to open. I told you she is perfect. I'm kind of seeing you judging me at this point, like what the hell is this supreme human being doing with this schmuck? Hahaha… Shut up, voice in my head; what are you talking about?

Okay, so back to reality. I am here at this moment in time staring at the most beautiful young woman.

She nods at me.

"Hey." That is the most I can say at this point in time.

My god, man, the first thing I say to her is 'hey'. Not even something as profound or elegant as 'oh, beautiful lady of the lake, how I wish this moment would never end and I stand before you a humble jester staring at the sun'. On second thought, 'hey' is better.

"Hey, Ajay. Dad, you know Ajay?" she says as she looks at me and then behind me.

A voice from behind me replies, "Hello, Ajay."

Yep, it is her dad. I turn to him and all I can think is… How long was he there behind me?

"Hello, Mr Singh. I did not see you there," I reply.

"Ajay, she needs to be back by 9:30pm," Mr Singh says as he walks into the house.

"Yes, sir," I reply nervously.

"Honestly, Dad, he has been walking me home from school since we were in primary school. There is no one in the world I am ever going to be safer with," replies Ria as she grabs my hand with both of her hands and walks towards the driveway.

The night is still, silent and clear. No clouds in the sky. It seems like every constellation in the world is visible in the night sky tonight. Well, not every constellation; that's an exaggeration, but the next part is not. The ground lights up like a street of gold as the light from the moon's rays shine brightly.

* * *

Ajay gazes upon me as we walk down the pathway to his car. I stare at Ajay, who is now fully focussed on the car door. I unhook my arm from Ajay's arm and grab the door handle before he manages to get it first. I am quick and always one step ahead.

"I can open the door; I have done this before, you know." I say sarcastically as he moves to the seat.

"I was being chivalrous," Ajay says in the sweetest way.

"Chivalrous!" I reply as I begin to laugh and give Ajay a look as if to tell him 'seriously, dude'. "Get in the car."

"Yes, ma'am," Ajay replies with a smirk as he walks around the car and begins to laugh with me.

We get into the car and drive off.

Ajay – how do I describe him? I know… perfect… just perfect. He is the sweetest, kindest person I have ever known, him and his thick black, Urkel-style glasses. He has always been there, my partner in crime, my Ajay. I knew I loved him since forever, ever since we first walked home from school all those years ago. I remember it as if it is happening in this very moment. Primary school – that is where this journey all began. The day that changed my whole world forever.

I remember it like it is happening at this moment.

It was the middle of June. Winter just began to show its true form. The winds were chilly and you could feel the chatter of your teeth as you walked outside. My face was numb from the icy cold wind. We live in a small town; mostly, you know everyone and everyone knows you too. I heard from Emily, who heard it from Jackie, who heard it from Candice, who… well, by now, you guessed that this was definitely, one hundred percent, not first-hand information. Anyway… Our school was going to be giving us free muffins. That's right; you heard it from me, Ria Singh. Everyone was going to get muffins that day. So, naturally, I was going to be first in line and I was determined to be there before everyone else. This was the only reason I was bolting across to school in the icy cold wind. Mind you, it was sunny out, but still cold. The weather always gets a bit warmer later. I was the first in line – told ya I would be here first. Picture this, me, Ria Singh, eight years old. I had pigtails and my white school dress on; yes, I know, God-awful, right? I looked like the old librarian, Miss Timothy, and she was like 90. Well, truth be told, she was younger, but that lady looked like she was 90, with white hair and wrinkles, and she also had that grandma-white jersey. Great, I am off track again… Anyway, back to me standing in the line – scratch that; front and centre in the line. I could smell the muffins. I stood there looking at all those muffins and there *she* was – Kaayla._Crap. Just my luck. It looked as if Kaayla was going to be handing out the muffins. I didn't like Kaayla – she was so annoying. Did I say I didn't like Kaayla? Well, I didn't and I knew the feeling was the same for her too. *Forget her,*

Ria. When do I get my muffins? I kept looking at the clock above the table on the wall; it reminded me of the one Nani had in her kitchen – great, off track again. I looked back at the clock – was it time yet? *Now… I think it is time…* Muffin time. It was muffin time. Miss Maharaj signalled to let everyone come to the table. I rushed to grab one and then look at a second. I went to grab a second one, but then I heard…

"Only one, Shorty," said Kaayla as she stared at me with her arms crossed and a look on her face that said 'don't test me'.

"But it's for someone else," I replied in a disappointed tone.

"Then they have to come get it themselves," replied Kaayla in an arrogant and rude tone.

"But… But… Miss Maharaj…" I looked at Miss Maharaj in the hope that she could help me get a second one. It was important that I got a second one. I waited for her to give me some sort of sign; I needed to get another one.

"I'm sorry, Ria. Just one per student," Miss Maharaj replied in a way that just crushed me to the deep parts of my soul.

I felt the last bit of hope rise from my body and hover there as it slowly disappeared into the air. I dragged my feet away from the table, with my head dropped to the floor. Disappointed, I walked away to the locker room. I got my school bag, put my muffin in my lunch box and placed my lunch box in my bag. I stared at my bag as I placed it back in my locker, and then looked at a boy standing in the corner of the room. He was just there – him and a very thick pair of glasses. *Hmmm…* I walked up to him. He looked at me with a very nervous expression.

"Hi, I'm Ria. Can I ask you a favour?" I asked him. Before he could answer, I continued, "See, I need your help. I want to use your glasses so I can get another muffin. See, it's very, very important, so very important, but I am in a bit of trouble, because Kaayla is over there and she is not much help. She won't let me have another… and it's very important."

Before I could finish, he took off his glasses and handed them to me. I put them on and then tied my pigtails together.

"How do I look?" I asked him.

"P-P-Perfect," he replied as I set off to get my second muffin.

I walked up to the table. By then, most of the students had got their muffins and there was no one in line again. I looked Kaayla right in her eyes, picked up another muffin and slowly walked away. She had no clue it was me. Yes, little old me, Ria Singh. I was a genius.

"Perfect. He was so right," I whispered as I headed back to my locker to get my bag. I opened the zipper and my lunch box was there, but the muffin was gone. "My muffin… What? Where's my muffin?" I asked.

I looked around and saw two boys running out of the building. I grabbed my bag and ran towards them. They must have it. They must be the ones who stole my muffin. Those evil little boys. Could they not understand how important it was? I mean, it took me two different tries to get those muffins. They could have been smarter than to just steal it from someone.

I went to the door and walked outside. There they were. The two boys were just standing there holding the muffin.

"Hey, that's mine!" I yelled at them as I pointed at my muffin.

As I got closer to grab the muffin from the boy, someone behind me grabbed the muffin I had in my hand and pushed me hard. I could only think of one thing at that moment and that was: *how much is this going to hurt?* I closed my eyes as I fell. I was falling, but I fell into someone.

"I got you," said the person.

I looked at his face, but I was still wearing the glasses. It was all a bit fuzzy. They were very thick glasses, but I knew that voice.

"Glasses?" I said as I took off the glasses and looked at him.

"*Ratty Ria!*" screamed a voice I knew all too well. It was Kaayla. She continued, "I knew it was you, you little *brat!* It's *one* per student, but now you get none."

Kaayla then took both muffins and smashed them on the floor with her foot.

"*That was important!*" I yelled.

She just continued to mock me.

One of the other boys rushed to grab me, but he got there first. He was not a very big kid and he was just around my height, but it did not matter in that moment as he tried to save me.

"Go through me first," he said as he moved forward. At that moment, I just knew – yes, that is when I knew.

"Fine, Four Eyes," said the other boy before he punched him so hard that he fell to the floor.

For a moment, I just looked at this boy lying on the floor and thought, *He is brave.*

As quickly as I could, I grabbed the boy on the floor and tried to pull him up so we could run. There was a time for a fight and there was a time to run and then was an awesome time to run. He stumbled up, but we managed to run away from Kaayla and her troop. We ran as fast as our little legs could carry us and we managed to get away from the school, but, more importantly, away from Kaayla and her goon squad. I wish I could say it was a win for us, but I lost the muffins. I lost the muffins. Disappointed once again, I lost another round to my enemy, Kaayla, but, as we ran, I realised I had an ally. No more fighting alone, I guessed, but could I ask that of him?

I handed him his glasses.

"You're bleeding," I said to him as I searched in my bag for my facecloth.

"Here, use this," I said to him as I handed him the facecloth.

He placed it on his nose as we walked.

He looked at me and, in a very sincere tone, said, "You didn't get the muffins."

I nodded at him in disappointment. "It was important," I said.

Without a second to think, he grabbed his bag, opened it and handed me two muffins.

"How?" I asked curiously. "You remember, it was one per student."

"No one sees me," he said.

I looked at him, grabbed his hand and pulled him with me.

* * *

We walked on the pathway until it turned into grass and then to no pathway at all. We got to the bottom of the bridge near the river. There was an old woman sitting near a fire and a cardboard shelter. She seemed to have been squatting there for years. I wondered how or what had caused her to be there. Ria took one of the muffins and went to the lady.

"Hey, Missy," she said as she handed her the muffin. "We brought you something. Have a beautiful day."

"You have a beautiful day too, young Miss Ria," the lady said with a smile, and she waved back at us as we walked back to the road.

"So what is the other muffin for?" I asked Ria as I looked at her.

"I like muffins too, Glasses," she replied.

"Ajay. My name is Ajay," I replied.

I knew that day… I just knew… as she broke the muffin in two pieces and handed me one piece… as we talked and laughed and I walked her home for the very first time. I just knew… how much I loved her.

* * *

We are here. I just look at Ria again. She is watching me from the passenger seat.

"We're here, Ajay," she says to me in a sarcastic tone.

"I know – I am driving, remember," I reply.

She glances back at me with a piercing look as she says, "Nice, Smarty."

She stares out the car window.

"The old drive-through. This place has been closed for a while now," she says as she looks at the cars in front of us.

"Not tonight. Tonight, for one night only, we get to relive watching…" I change my tone to one much deeper. "*Creature from the Black Lagoon.*"

"Do you remember when we snuck in and hid near the projector room and watched it?" Ria recalls our misadventures from our childhood.

One day of many like it – we almost got caught so many times over the years. We would sit either under the window or under the staircase deck. Those were fun times, as both of us loved movies and, more than that, we loved every moment we spent with each other.

"Ha! Yeah, I do. My mother whipped me for that – that still hurts, but I loved every moment of it. That was worth any amount of punishment that followed. I got to spent those moments with you," I reply.

Her eyes begin to sparkle and get bigger as we drive to a parking spot where we can see the screen running old trailers for all the movies we would sneak in to watch.

I hear a song on the radio in the car next to us. As I turn to Ria, it begins to play the chorus of *The Flamingos' I Only Have Eyes for You.* Sounds cheesy and corny, right, but those words mean so much more with her right here, right now. Her here with me.

Ria looks me dead in the eye. I pause for a second. She continues to look me in the eyes. Is she going to kiss me? Is this our first kiss? She moves in closer. It is…. Oh my God, it is! Our first kiss and this corny sound is playing in the background….

Shut up, mind.

She is leaning in…

"Popcorn," she says, still staring me in the eyes.

"Popcorn?" I ask. Not a first kiss. Just popcorn.

"Yeah, we need popcorn," she states like a kid in a candy store. Her eyes light up and she smirks.

"With butter," I reply.

Great, now she has got me excited for popcorn. She always has that effect on me.

* * *

He gets out of the car and heads to the store in the back of the lot.

I, on the other hand, just sit here in the car, thinking. I was so close. I should have just kissed him. Anyway… I look around. There are a few people I think I know. I turn to my right. Oh shoot! Is that the police captain and his wife?

Ria, just sink a little lower in the seat, I say to myself as I slowly sink lower into the seat.

He did not see you. Maybe he doesn't even remember you. Yeah right – you think that man is ever going to forget that you managed to slug his niece on graduation?

That's right – on graduation day.

Well, she did deserve it; you don't mess with my Ajay. Anyway, the movie is about to begin. Where is he?

I look towards the store. I see Ajay. He is cornered by… You have got to be kidding me. Really, does it have to be her? Obviously, it had to be. It is Kaayla and her dickhead boyfriend; I can't remember his name – S… D… Never mind. They have always had an issue with us. I get out of the car.

* * *

"Hey, Four Eyes. Where's Ratty Ria?" Kaayla demands.

Kaayla is now much older, but seems to have grown even meaner with time. Man, why does it have to be this psycho? Why tonight? Does this crazy person just stalk Ria on a regular basis? This rivalry has been going on for more than a decade. Someone clearly has a lot of issues.

"I don't know," I say as I stare at the two people in front of me.

I am boxed in between them and the wall behind me. I have two popcorn buckets in my hand and I am now in a defensive stance. I am a master of defending myself. I am using the buckets as a shield, but Kaayla's boyfriend is much larger than I am. He looks like a rugby player on steroids even though he is about five-foot-eight. Makes sense, right? Beasts are supposed to be with their own kind.

Shit, Ajay, you sound like Ria. Shit – Ria!

I have to get rid of these two before she sees them. I try to look over to the car, but try to watch these two as well.

"Look, babe, he has two boxes with him," the dickhead says.

I know, but for the life of me I can't remember his name. Was it S… or D…? Yeah, D sounds right – Dickhead. Also, surprise, surprise – it can count to two; that must be a great accomplishment for that Neanderthal.

"*Where is she, you pathetic waste?*" screams Kaayla.

My god, she must have been born a banshee.

"I don't know. I am here with my mum, okay," I reply as her boyfriend grabs one of the boxes and throws the popcorn in my face before pushing me to the wall.

"*Speak, nerd!*" he yells.

I am trapped. I am trapped. I close my eyes as he balls up his hand and pulls back. All I can think of is not how much this is going to hurt, but more about what the aftermath of Ria finding out is going to be. I picture a night spent in lock-up and her dad looking at me and just shaking his head, and there are those two both with broken noses and ripped clothing, and Ria in the cell next to me with that goofy grin.

"*Hey!*" a voice echoes.

As the guy turns, he is hit hard right on the nose; it immediately drops him to his knees. He grabs his nose, but blood begins to pour from between his fingers and streams down his fingers and his face.

He yells, "Aargh!"

Kaayla runs to her boyfriend and someone grabs my hand. As I open my eyes, I am pulled with haste. It's Ria. We run to find some cover behind one of the empty cars in the lot before the apes get back up and chase us once again. This night has not gone the way I was hoping. The only action we have got was someone's broken nose. Guess those karate lessons have paid off for Ria.

Ria and I are seated on the floor next to a car. Hey… I remember this car. It's a lot rustier than before. This car has been in this lot even before we attended. Ria peeks through the car windows and looks at Kaayla and her boyfriend. They are now searching the parking lot for us. They are headed away, more towards the other cars in the lot.

"You okay?" we both utter at the same time and then nod back at each other.

"Your mum?" she say curiously as she looks at me.

"I panicked," I reply.

"Seriously, your mum," she says as she begins to laugh a bit.

I hand her the bucket of popcorn that survived the ordeal by some random luck of the universe. We sit there munching the popcorn as we wait for the vengeful duo to leave the parking lot.

I look up to see if I can see them, but notice that the movie is now already halfway through. There goes movie night. We have been hiding here for almost fifty minutes. Those two should have given up by now. Ria and I very cautiously walk towards the car, looking around us at every corner and turn. We stand in front of my car. She just looks at me. The tyres have been slashed. I take a deep breath and just let out a mild sigh.

"I'm sorry," Ria says as she grabs my hand with both her hands.

* * *

"Guess we are walking home tonight," says Ajay with that sincere tone of his.

I always wonder if anything truly bothers him. His life would have been so much easier if we never met in the first place. I cannot express how badly I feel that all of this was because of petty schoolyard rivalry that, to this day, has not ended. As we begin to walk, I look back once more at the movie playing in the background. This was supposed to be a perfect night, but once again, thanks to the witch and me and our stupid childish behaviour, all of this became the perfect nightmare instead. I truly did want to see the end of the movie and I wanted that slow drive home and I wanted that awkward silence we would have sitting in the car looking around and watching the night sky before one of us tried to kiss the other. Our first kiss – that is how this night was supposed to end, but instead, most of the evening was spent with a broken nose and running. I will get Kaayla back for this… but that is what has got us here in the first place. Neither one of us wants the other one to win, and we will continue to upstage each other. The casualty of this war between two rivals is always the people close to us. In my case, it will always be Ajay.

"What the hell is that guy's name?" he asks as he looks at me.

"I can't remember. I think it starts with S or D," I say.

As I am about to say the next word, he says it with me.

"Dickhead!"

We begin to laugh and, just like that, it seems as if the whole world is normal again. It will always be better, because he is there with me.

As we continue to walk home, we joke about the past and all the crazy stuff we got into. You know, like the time we stole the glasses of the statue in the park. I still have that thing in my room somewhere… or the time we spent the entire day at the library telling the librarian that we needed a book on witches and their relationship to Kaayla – haha!

We reach the door. The door that began this journey. The door that we ended up at every day after school and every night after college. The nerves are now all gone. The air still lingers with the sound of our laughter. Here we are, two souls standing on this beautiful porch. I get a little closer to him and he also moves closer to me. I stare at his eyes through his glasses. He has beautiful hazel eyes. As I stare deeply into his eyes, the world around me fades into the darkness of the night. The darkness that surrounds us is enveloped by a hue of orange and red. I can feel my heart racing. Am I nervous? No. This is a good feeling. This feels like the moment has slowly stopped time. The air no longer lingers with the sound of laugher; it has become too intense.

I see it. I can feel it. He steps forward and leans closer to me. This is it – our first kiss. I lean closer to him, but the door begins to open. Ajay moves like lightning and steps back.

So close… Urgh, that was so close.

The door fully opens and there is my father.

"Dad," I say to him.

"Earlier than expected," says my dad as he turns to Ajay.

"Car trouble, sir," Ajay replies as he steps down a step on the porch.

I look at him and can't help but wonder what our first kiss would have been like.

Thanks, Dad, for your impeccable timing.

All I needed was just two minutes – okay, maybe five. Alas, this remains an interlude for now.

"Did you have any fun?" my father asks.

How ironic, I think as I look at Ajay and then at my dad.

"Yes, Dad." I look back at Ajay with that smile on his face as he nods back at me.

"Goodnight," Ajay says as he goes down another step.

"Goodnight," I quickly reply, not thinking anything of it at this moment.

I should never have been so quick to say goodnight. I should have asked him to come in. I should have told him to sit with me on the porch a little while. I should have… but… but I did not. How could I have known? If only I did know that this night would change our lives so much. I would not have let him walk away.

As he walks away, he waves at me one last time and I wave back before I close the door. He fades away into the bushes.

* * *

The doorbell rings multiple times. It sounds like when church bells ring. Each ring sounds ominous, as if it is a foreboding warning striking each time to remind you, the reader, of how much danger lurks within its calls. The doorbell rings again, but this time it is followed by someone banging on the door frantically. My father opens the door and Ajay's mum rushes in. I am still groggy as I walk down the hallway to the door. She is frantic, hysterical and crying. I can hear parts of her screams and anguish. I am now closer to the door. I can see Ajay's mum, but cannot make out what she is saying. She is yelling and crying. My dad is there and he is trying to calm her, but she continues to cry and yell. At this moment, all I can think is, *Where is Ajay?*

As I get closer to her, she grabs me tightly and hugs me, and she is now crying harder. I hug her back. She says something; I still cannot make out what. Hold on a minute… Did she just say…?

No, no, no, she didn't…

At this moment, I don't want to believe it.

No… Nooo… Nooo… not Ajay.

She did not say…

I listen to her voice as it begins to get clearer. I still remember those words. Those dreadful words.

"Ajay is missing, Ria. My Ajay is lost."

Those words echo through my soul repeatedly as I hear the word 'missing' over and over. How can he be missing? No, he can't be. I just saw him last night. He waved at me. That is the last thing I remember of him. Him and his goofy glasses. He waved at me. He waved at me before he walked home. He cannot be… not Ajay. No… not my Ajay.

I feel a chill run through my body. This is not a chill you feel on a cold winter day. It is as if my soul has frozen in the icy depths of the Antarctic. This coldness and darkness are felt far deeper into the deepest part of my soul. My world has been completely and devastatingly destroyed. I cannot move at all.

The only thing I can do is scream as loud as I can, "Not Ajay!" I hold onto Ajay's mum even tighter as I cry with her.

Not my Ajay… He is not lost… No… No, he is out there… He is just playing a prank… No… No, that's my thing. Mr Serious would never… not unless I was part of it. The cries continue as the police arrive.

* * *

The darkness has shrouded the room with an intense despair. The tears have run dry, but the stains of the pain still linger as we are all in the kitchen. I slowly look at Ajay's mum; her head is down, with her hands on her head. She is whispering a mantra over and over. I cannot make out what she is saying, but I now understand. She is praying for Ajay to walk through the door and just say that he was safe and he was home again. The police are still around the house and my dad is talking to Detective Wills. I feel so helpless at this point. It has been more than two hours since the knock at the door. I cannot take it anymore. I have to do something; anything will be better than just sitting here and staring at this table. I get up and grab my jacket. My dad looks at me and then back at the detective.

"Ria," he says as he looks at me heading to the door.

"Yes, Dad?" I reply.

"Where are you going?" he asks, but he knows.

"I can't just sit here. Ajay is out there somewhere," I say as I get closer to the kitchen door.

"The police are doing all they can to find Ajay. You need to rest and look over there," my dad says as he nods at Ajay's mum. "Look at her; do you not think she wants to be out there too?"

"I know, Dad, but it can't hurt if I am there with them. Do you think that if it was me who was out there all alone and with no one with me, would Ajay not be out there looking for me?" My emotions begin to get the better of me. I stare at my dad and then look at the wall as the tears roll down my cheeks. "I won't let her down and I won't let him down. You can refuse and you can say whatever you need to, but I am going out there and I will find him."

My father looks at the detective and then my mum sitting on the couch in the far corner. He grabs his coat.

"Let's go," he says as he walks to me.

I nod back at him, the stream of tears still rolling down my cheeks. I still have hope that Ajay is out there and I will get him back.

We search for hours until the morning. I don't remember much about returning home. I fall asleep as we drive around and my dad carries me back into the house. My mum is up at that time.

"Did you find him?" she asks.

My dad looks at me in his arms and just shakes his head in disappointment, or so that is what my brother said at the time. I wake up at around 11am, jump up and rush into the kitchen, only to see my mum and Ajay's mum still sitting there and no Ajay around. My excitement turns back into a nightmare. The night was real and he is missing.

* * *

The town rallies together for the first few weeks as we search every field and forest in town. Most days were there same. I move my zombified body through the tall grass and trees. Lost, I now really understand what it means to be truly lost in search of something I love more than life itself. It feels like two souls were lost that night and now everyone is in search of the one half that will reignite my soul back to its default settings. Every moment I look around and hope that it is me who finds him. That he will be just standing there and I will walk up to him and tell him that I love him and that he is such an arsehole for disappearing, and then I will hug him and tell him I love him again and again. How I wish more than anything right now that, on the next turn or next to the next tree, there he will be, but it is never the case. I can feel myself lose a part of me just one bit at a time. My smile has vanished and all that is left is a cloud that surrounds my soul like a never-ending storm that keeps pouring down onto me constantly, no matter what I do and how much hope I have left. It is beginning to feel hopeless.

We comb acres of land, inch by inch. Every night, I sit at the dinner table after hours of searching just staring at my parents and Ajay's mum as I play around with my food. Every time, I stare at the front door with the last glimmer of hope that I have that day. I pray that the doorbell will ring at this moment and it will be Ajay ringing it, but it doesn't happen. I just keep staring at the door, hoping.

There is pain; I am trying to understand this pain. It is in my chest. I cannot explain this feeling. I have a sort of burning sensation, but it is not as if I am on fire; just a warm feeling that I can feel someone there. I can feel him there. He is out there and I know he is or maybe that is just my imagination. Maybe I… Maybe… Maybe… My thoughts continue as I slowly wake up in my chair, still staring at the door. The intensity of the pain grows stronger as I walk closer to the door. It is as if I anticipate the door to ring with every step I take. I end up at my door. I dread to open this door. This feeling of loneliness and the emptiness drapes onto me like a blanket over my body. I open the door to my room with a heavy heart and an even heavier sense of dread. This feeling has now overshadowed my earlier feelings of hope and optimism.

I slowly walk to the edge of my bed and flop my lifeless body onto the bed, crashing into the sheets like a rock into water. I stare at the ceiling. I am so tired, but I cannot fall asleep; my mind is racing at a million miles a second. Did we check in the barn at the Williams farm? Did we check the bridge? Did we...? Did we...? I just want to scream at this moment. I just want to be rid of these dark emotions that I am feeling. It is strangling me with every passing moment. I can't breathe. I... I... I take a deep breath. I can't stop the tears and they flow like a river, rushing down my cheeks. Why does this hurt so much? I love him. That's why.

"Bastard," I whisper.

All I can think at this moment is, *Where are you? Are you safe there? Please be safe.*

Dear God, I... I have not asked you for anything before. Please let my Ajay be safe and return him to me. Please, God; that is all I ask for.

I just lie here in tears. I can hear my parents arguing about how unhealthy my behaviour has become over the past few days and that I should see a professional. I can hear them less and less with each passing moment. The emotions are drowning out the world around me. It feels as if I am slowly dying on the inside. The hope is still there, but its flame is slowly fading. The cold grasp of this depressive state has grown unbearable. My rational thought... Rational... The rational part is falling away. I cannot think anymore. All I want is to feel alive again. I want so desperately to feel that warmth again. I just want to see his face and that smile. I just want to see that smile once more. I promise I will never let him go again. I will grab onto him and never let him go. I miss his Urkel glasses.

The coldness in my heart grows colder as days turn to weeks and weeks turn to months.

CHAPTER TWO

Sometimes They Come Back

It has been more than six months. The search for Ajay has all but died down from the people in the city. My condition has not got any better over the months. I see a psychiatrist on a weekly basis. The coldness and emptiness has not faded away, but the hope has not died either. Every night, I go out, still with the hope of finding Ajay. I yearn more now to see that face, although now it seems like a distant memory. I will not give up on Ajay. I have dedicated my entire savings to hire a private investigator to search for him. I know that it will take more than just a private investigator to find him. I walk through the old trails in the woods, reminiscing about the days when we played in the fields behind the wheat farms. There is an old red barn that still stands today, but it has seen better days. It was rundown and make a lot of creaking noises. I don't know why, but I was constantly drawn back to that barn. Maybe it's because, whenever we played hide and seek, Ajay hid in there. I desperately hope that he is there. I space out often and land up in front of an old chest that sits on the second floor. I open it and, as I do, I pray to whichever God will listen to me.

"Please, I will do anything. Whatever you want. Please let him be in here," I plead every time.

I beg the gods for his return. Good, bad or whatever may come. I just want to see him, but alas, my pleas go unheard and my faith is now lost. How could they take him away? I begin to question those who say it is God's will.

Why him, God? Why my Ajay? Why not the person who is the reason he is gone in the first place?

The world would be a better place if I was gone and not him. What have I ever done to still be here while he is gone? The best I can ever do is cause more trouble and heartache for everyone in my life. My hope is on its last stand, but I will not give up on him even if, since last week, everyone else has. They buried an empty casket, because there was no Ajay to cremate. How do you give up on him like that when you have not found him yet?

I did not go to that farce. Family and friends say I should move on that he is no more. I can still feel a part of him at times before the darkness shrouds that hope, but I will not give up on him. I keep playing it in my mind. If I had not got into trouble by knocking out Dickhead. They would not have slashed his tyres and we would not have walked home and he would have driven home safely. No… No… I should not have got him to go for popcorn in the first place… then no Kaayla and no Dickhead. If only… If only… I start to cry again.

No, Ria. You have to be stronger.

He is still out there. I feel him.

I hear my dad come through the door. It's just us here. My mum is out with Ajay's mum. I greet my dad and head to my room. I stand there like every other day just as I have before, but, unlike the days before, I don't feel the loneliness and the emptiness. I stare at the door, but something feels different. I can feel it. I cannot explain this weird sensation that has come over me, but it feels so much lighter. I open the door.

There he is.

This can't be…

I am looking directly at him and I still… I must be seeing things.

The stress and depression has manifested Ajay in front of me. This must be a dream; this is not possible. Why would he not just come through the door like a normal person?

How would he have got into my room in the first place? I look at the presence before me and I can see it is him, but he is facing the wall at the far corner of my room. What is he wearing? Why is he in a black jumpsuit?

"Ajay!" I call to him as he turns towards me.

He looks very pale – no glasses. I have never seen him like that before. He looks different, but not just in appearance; his presence and aura seem different as well. He smiles at me.

"Ria," he says as I go closer to him.

I place my hand on his cheek and gaze into his eyes. The tears roll down my cheeks; I cannot get over the excitement of seeing Ajay.

I've found him. I've found him.

Well, actually, he found her. After all those days and nights searching frantically. Every sleepless night finally makes sense in that moment when I stare deep into his eyes.

"You bastard. You utter bastard," I manage to utter.

I stare deeper into Ajay's eyes with a fire and desire I have never felt before. My emotions are running wild. I'm excited to see him, but, as I look into his eyes, I am also apprehensive.

"I love you, Ajay," I say.

* * *

I stare back into Ria's eyes. Something within me just says to grab her. I grab her waist and pull her closer. Our lips are so close.

I whisper back to her, "I love you more."

Our lips lock together as I kiss her passionately as we embrace. This is our first kiss and it is exactly everything I ever imagined.

There is a voice at the back of my mind. *Tell her to leave, Ajay. She needs to leave, Ajay, before… before it's…*

I keep ignoring it. This voice is getting louder. I continue to try to ignore it over and over again. My hand is on her face and we are still kissing.

I ask myself, *What is that smell? What is that beautiful smell?*

It smells like that moment after the rain on a summer day.

Why am I so famished?

The intense feeling of hunger keeps growing stronger, and so does the voice. *Tell her to go,* it repeats.

I begin to kiss Ria on her cheek and now I move down to her neck. The smell is getting stronger. I am starving, but I have missed seeing Ria for so long. I am still starving; it must be because I haven't eaten in a while. The voice is now yelling at me. The noise inside my head has become unbearable. It is yelling, *Tell her to go! Don't do it!*

Do what? What am I not supposed to do, voice in my head? What can be so devastating that I should not do it? I am still kissing her on her neck, but that smell and the hunger is getting stronger. I have never felt so hungry in my entire life. I should just…

"Ajay! Ajay! *Ajay!*" screams Ria.

My grip on her is much tighter. I hold her as if I am grabbing onto her for dear life. My teeth are in her neck. I cannot stop. I cannot stop.

"Ajay, *stop!*" yells the voice.

Ria is trying to fight me off, but she cannot. I can faintly hear her screams – 'Ajay, stop! Argh!' – as she slowly fades away. I watch as she fades and I am now desperate to pull away from her. I finally get enough courage to push her away and watch as her limp body falls to the floor.

"What the *hell* have I done?" I utter in total disbelief. "What the hell has happened to me?"

I am all over the place; my emotions are running at a high. I focus back on where I am. I am in Ria's room. Okay, I am in Ria's room. I saw Ria. Right… Yes, I saw Ria. I saw Ria… The realisation hits. I kissed Ria… and my focus is now on Ria lying on the floor. She is still breathing, but barely. I rush to her, but the smell and hunger get strong again as I move closer to her. I try to force myself away from her.

"*Ria!*" I scream.

Ria slowly opens her eyes and stares back at me. My mouth is covered in her blood. She begins to cry on the floor. I stare at her in horror as I watch the love of my life writhing in pain. I feel so helpless at the moment. I try to step forward to hold her, but, every time, I have to hold myself back as the hunger draws me to her neck again. I cannot hold back, but I have to. The pain of seeing her there lying in blood and crying in pain… I continue to pull myself away. Ria's cries slowly become screams of pain. I can see her teeth are now longer than before.

"What have I done?" I ask myself. *What have I done, indeed? What is wrong with me?*

You should have let her go, says the voice in my head.

"*Ria!*" I scream again.

"It burns inside, Ajay. It burns inside!" Ria cries, in agony.

I can see her skin melting and there is smoke coming off her skin. Her skin begins to liquefy and the melded ooze of blood, plasma and skin begins to roll down her body like melted ice cream on a hot summer day. Her insides begin melting away on the floor. I stand here. I just stand here… I cannot move. I am just trying to fight the hunger and trying to get to Ria at the same time. I stand watching as the most important person in my life, my Ria, disintegrates in front of me. I am helpless. I stand up and hear father's voice coming towards the room. Mr Singh enters the room and sees Ria on the floor. He rushes to her. Ria is still screaming in agony as she is slowly dying a painful death. I still stand here invisible to him.

"*Ria!*" he yells.

"I failed, Mr Singh. I failed to protect her from myself," I whisper as I see him grab Ria's remains.

* * *

I am running with no direction, but, no matter how fast I run, I realise I cannot outrun this moment that keeps haunting me. I can see her… Ria. I can see Ria's face. The horror in her. The horror in her eyes.

What have I done?

I am feeling lost. I feel empty. I feel incomplete without her.

What have I done?

I warned you, the voice cries out. *I warned you.*

"I did not understand you," I whisper back to the voice.

You were foolish! I told you to get her out of there.

The voice echoes those words that run deep into my soul.

But I missed Ria. I did not know who to go to. She means everything to me. She is my life, I retort.

And now Ria's gone, the voice yells.

I stop dead in my tracks. I stop running, because I have come to the realisation that I can never outrun what I have done. I stand here just staring into the distance. I see her… but this is not the Ria I remember. This is the Ria… I cannot unsee this. This is her when she was melting in front of me. I stare at her. I can see her, with her skin still melting away as she tries to scream as she reaches for me, her arms stretched out… and then I hear a deathly scream echo around me. I close my eyes. That is not my Ria. She was never like that. That is not my Ria. I take a deep breath and slowly open my eyes. There is no one here, but I look around and wonder… *Where am I?*

Railroad tracks. I am standing on a railroad track. I can hear water – a stream or river maybe. This place feels familiar. I know this place. I am on the railway tracks. Things are a bit fuzzy. I remember… Why is time so fuzzy? This place… This place, I remember. I know this place.

Huh… It's the bridge over the river. I walk to the edge of the bridge. I see her over and over again, but time is so fuzzy. *How did I get here? Where am I?*

On the bridge, moron. You are on the bridge. It is night. You killed her, says the voice.

The night… That night… I remember. Every time I see her face, I see that night.

Yes, the night you killed her, says the voice.

No… No… I remember her face. I remember looking into her eyes. I remember we kissed.

Yes, the night you killed her, says the voice again.

No… No… the night we almost kissed. I remember now.

The door opened; Mr Singh was there. I remember stepping back.

"Dad," says Ria.

"Earlier than expected," says Mr Singh as he turns to me.

"Car trouble, sir," I reply as I slowly move down a step on the porch.

"Did you have any fun?" asks Mr Singh.

I look at Ria.

She looks back at me and then at her dad and says, "Yes, Dad."

She looks back at me. I smile at her and nod. All I can think of is how beautiful she looks. I want to kiss her. I really want to kiss her.

"Goodnight," I utter as I move one step lower.

"Goodnight," Rai replies fast.

I move toward the pathway.

I wish that, in that moment, I did not. Something was going to change everything for us. If only I asked her to sit with me for a while. If only… but our path was always set.

I waved at her and she waved back before closing the door.

The night is peaceful and calm like many nights before. I walked home this way many times before. It is just eight houses down. There is no one in sight as I walk tonight.

But there was, says the voice.

I am trying to remember. I need to remember, because… because all of this is my fault. I should never have… I should never have… Why is it so hard to remember? I should never have… What the hell was it?

I am walking home. A breeze shakes some of the trees and it startles me, so I look up, but there is nothing there. I turn back to head home and there she is. A woman stands in front of me.

How could I forget her face? Why can I not remember?

She looks like one of those models in TV commercials. You know, blue eyes and blonde.

"Hey," I say to her.

"Hey to you too," she replies as she stares at me in a very weird way.

"Are you lost? I have not seen you around here before," I say a bit nervously.

It is the way she looks at me.

"I just got into town. My car broke down a few houses down that way." She points. "Can you help me get to a phone?"

I know what you are thinking. Stop. Remember, I was 22 and I did not know any better.

"You're in luck; my house is just five houses away," I say as I begin to walk home.

The lady accompanies me. The breeze picks up again and rustles the trees, and I look up again.

"Do you hear that?" I ask her as we walk to my house.

"Don't mind him. He's just having some fun," she replies.

Her words send a chill down my spine. At this point in time, I am too afraid to look back at her. My breathing gets heavier and I am still looking at the trees. I can see it. It's… It's huge! I turn to her and look her in the eyes.

"What the fuck?" I exclaim as she grabs me and pushes me onto the tree.

She moves closer and sinks her fangs into my neck. My breathing gets heavier and faster. What is going on? I am trying to scream, but cannot. What is going on? I am slowly fading and I am about to pass out. I see it — this huge monster, no less than seven feet tall, and it has wings. Its face is cat-like, but with no whiskers, and it has sharp fangs on both sides of its jaw and wings with feathers. I struggle to keep my eyes open. I feel so drained of life. As I drift off, the beast grabs both of us and… I think… I am not sure, but I think we are flying. I can feel the wind in my hair and their fangs in my neck.

I don't remember much more than that. I need to remember more. The time is so fuzzy. I remember this black jumpsuit… I remember a room. Yes, a room… a basement, I think. I cannot be sure, but some sort of room. I escaped, but how? Why did I escape? I shake my head. Time is so fuzzy. I escaped… *How?*

Things are still so fuzzy. I remember a name. What is it again? A… A… Alina. Who is Alina? What does she have to do with this room? Why can't I remember?

Focus, says the voice.

I am trying to. Hydro dam… I remember a hydro dam, but what does that have to do with things? I remember walking past a store with TVs in it. I remember one of the stations showing the date – June 1991.

June 1991? That can't be – it is 28 November 1990. June 1991… I feel cold – cold and hungry – but my mind is only focussed on one thing: Ria. I have to see Ria. I keep picturing her face on the day on the porch. I have to see Ria. I have to see Ria.

Once again, time feels so fuzzy. I just remember wanting her so badly. I just had to see her.

I am now outside her house. I see Mr Singh go into the house.

I just want to see her.

Don't, *says the voice.*

"I have to," I whisper.

The time is so fuzzy… and now I am in her room.

How did I get here? The door opens. There she is. She smells so good.

"Ajay," she says.

I turn to her and smile.

"Ria," I say as she moves closer to me.

The smell is stronger and she looks so beautiful. I must be in Heaven at this moment.

I killed her… I know I am here on this bridge at this moment in time… and I killed her; that is what I know. The time is not fuzzy in this moment; I am on the edge of this bridge looking down at the rocks below. The coldness is growing in me once again. I feel emptiness; it is clawing inside me, scratching away at the fabric of my soul. The emptiness desperately wants to get out and consume this universe. The hunger will soon follow. It is a long way down. I stare at the ground below and lose focus of the world around me. Ajay… I step closer to the edge of the bridge. I look at the horizon and there, in the distance, I see the darkened sky turn a dark blood red. The sun is about to rise.

Vampires die by sunlight, right? Oh, now you are silent… No voice in my head at this point. *I would love to hear your advice now. Still silent?*

I look down again. Without another thought, I close my eyes and leap off the bridge in a swan dive. I cannot believe what pops into my head as I am falling. The one thought I should have had was… *What the hell are you doing? Trying to kill yourself, moron.*

The fall is too quick, but I feel nothing… just emptiness. I can smell a musty, wet, earthy smell. I feel the soil underneath my face. I should be dead, but I am not. I push myself up to my knees and look at myself. No scratches, no blood and no broken bones. I should be dead. The orange hue in the distance catches my eye. The sun… There is still time. All the horror movies say that the sun should be able to kill a vampire, right? The sun will kill me. I crack my neck back into place as I sit and stare death in the face.

Oh! Joy, bringeth the sun's rays! I wish to bask in its wisdom.

I sit and wait for the first rays to bring tears and burning pain.

The death of a vampire is upon us, lads.

The sun's rays begin stalking the ground before me. They begin to devour the sand particles, one by one, laying its bright light upon each grain of sand. The sun's rays inch closer to me. Like a predator to its prey, the rays pounces on me.

"I embrace thee, death, and I will join you soon, my love," I say as the light strikes my body, but alas, I still remain.

How anticlimactic. I just sit here, confused. Do vampires not die from sunlight? Are they really vampires? Maybe it was a dream. The memory is still fuzzy and feels like it is a dream, but it's not. Ria is still gone, so this is definitely not a dream, but more like a never-ending nightmare.

I stand here with the sun beating down on my skin. It feels like it will be an extremely hot day. I am still unsure what is going on. Why am I still alive? Are that lady and the beast not vampires?

This thought continues to rattle in my head. I stand here just staring directly into the sun. Maybe I was never missing in the first place. Ria and I sat there on the porch that night. We joked about Kaayla and Dickhead. We spent the entire night just there, but, if that was real and these moments never happened, then, voice in my head, explain to me why I am here, no longer under the bridge. I now stand in front of a tombstone with my name on it. Why does it state 'Beloved son and best friend'? Why?

No… we are still on that porch. I will not accept this as my fate. I will not accept this as our fate. Destiny cannot be so cruel as to lead us together finally only for the two of us to be torn apart in such a gruesome fashion. So I do not accept the fate that was given to me. I will…

You have no choices, Ajay, says the voice. *Your path has been already set.*

"*No!*" I yell as I watch from the top of the hill, surrounded by tombstones as the hearse and a string of cars head towards the crematorium.

The time feels so fuzzy. It is like I can feel those moments when we were back on the walk home on that night, but now I drift between that time and this time. This one feels weird to me; it does not feel real, but that punch felt real, when I punched Dickhead; that felt like reality and this just feels like a dream state. The time feels so fuzzy. I close my eyes and now I stand at a distance watching as everyone is in the crematorium. I can see Mr Singh sitting next to the coffin. There is a picture of Ria next to the coffin. Mr Singh looks so lost. I just want to go to them and tell them how sorry I am and that I never meant to hurt her. I loved her.

I move forward slowly, but stop. I can't do this. This is not the right time. No matter what I say, it will never make this right.

Something can, says the voice.

"What?" I ask the voice in my head.

Kill the thing that made you this way, the voice replies.

I begin to wonder if this can truly set me free. I ponder if it is like the movies and the books. You know, kill the lead vampire and the curse breaks and you walk out with your life returning to normal. Is it possible? Am I even a vampire in the first place? The voice was right before; I should have listened, but I did not and now I am here.

I slowly step back, but someone grabs my arm. It feels familiar in a way. It feels like when Ria would grab my arm and then hold onto me. It feels like those days we walked home from school. There's a hand there. I turn to look at the hand on my arm. This hand looks familiar. I hesitate, but then raise my head to see the person's face. The scars and melting skin are still there; however, she looks a lot more like the Ria I knew before. In this moment, I remember a song we love from the band *Within Temptation* that speaks about being haunted by the memory of a loved one.

I feel a blanket of peacefulness come over me. This feels different to the other night. She turns to me. The weather turns from sunny and bright to gloomy, cold and dark. The area begins to freeze and the wind howls around us. I blink and she is gone. The time is so fuzzy. One minute, I am here, and then I am not. It is night. It is dark and I am now standing before a chain-link fence. I look around and it seems like I know this place. I am at what looks like an old dam. I can see myself and I am stumbling around trying to escape. I can feel my pain and confusion. I just want to see her. I see myself pass where I stand now. The time still feels fuzzy; it is as if I can see the past and present at the same time. There are two soldiers standing at the chain-link fence. I am standing a few metres away from them, but they do not see me. I think I am getting a good grasp of these powers. Why am I here?

I need their help.

Something inside me yells, *They can help kill the one who turned you!*

Can they really? I should just trust you, voice in my head.

It was not wrong before. I just stand here.

The voice yells once more, *Stay away from them!*

I can smell them. *Argh!* The hunger again… Need to focus. What was the name?

Alina, moron, says the voice.

Something has got an attitude.

I catch a glimpse of the blood-red hue on the horizon; it is almost dawn. I make myself visible to the soldiers and they immediately point their weapons at me. It is as if they knew I was here, but waited for me to make the first move.

"*Halt!*" they yell.

"I am here to see A– Alina," I say as I try to remember her name.

One of the soldiers fires a few rounds at me. The bullets strike my body, but just fall to the ground.

"I've tried that," I say, annoyed by these so-called soldiers.

The two soldiers look at each other in shock and awe.

One of the soldiers turns to me and says, "Those were vamp–"

"*Hold up!*" says a voice, but it is not the voice in my head.

CHAPTER THREE

Sometimes They Fade Away

Hold up… Can we just pause for a second here? I am going to take over the narrative of this story, so I call bullshit on the last few pages. So this so-called soldier shot at a vampire and the vampire did not move or even get hurt. Now I know what you are thinking. What the fuck is going on? At this point, you just nodded a bit, right? Maybe not or you are just as confused as I am. By now, you realise that I am not Ajay or the voice in his head, nor am I Ria. My name is… Hmmm, on second thought, maybe that is not important right now. What is important is the journey Ajay is now on. I am here to give this story a different point of view; we get to change the angle of this story just a bit. So what do we know right now? Ajay is not quite all there at this time. He seems like he is fighting his mind on where he is, but more importantly is *when* he is. His mind is a mess and he cannot keep track of the timeline. We will continue to journey between his point of view, Ria's point of view and possibly my point of view of the story. This is also the point in the story we find out a few pieces of the story that were overlooked or muddled in Ajay's mind. He has forgotten or, more likely, omitted a lot of his narrative of this story.

Where are we now? Right now, we are with Ajay and he has decided to go back to this facility. There he is. You can see him standing in front on the chain-link fence and the soldiers are pointing their weapons at him. The sun is still rising in the distance. Why here? This is where he woke up after his six-month ordeal. This place is the only other thing he remembers after his life-altering experience. He was in a comma – no, that's the wrong word. Com… Coma… Sorry, the word is coma. He was in a coma. Sorry, once again; English is not my first language. Anyway, the suicidal maniac standing before the soldiers is someone who has taught me so much; most of what I learnt has come from Ajay and a professor I once knew.

Let us back up just a tad. Before this scene unfolded, before our very imaginations and the time Ajay was depressed and contemplating death under the bridge – we are about 24 hours between those moments. I am going to let him tell you this part as best as he can, but don't worry; I am going to be here if things seem out of place. So, Ajay, you were at the bottom of the bridge, sitting in the mud with the sun striking your body. You sat there confused and still in a state of dark contemplation.

* * *

"No," I whisper as the tears begin to roll down my cheeks. The drops fall to the ground rapidly. I cannot understand how and why I am still alive.

"No. No. *No, no, nooooooo!*" What begins as whispers turn violently into yells to the gods as I look to Heaven above and echo my displeasure at my fate. "*Why am I alive?*"

I sit there in disbelief at my current situation. The logical part of my brain begins to run through every possibility. Maybe I am not a vampire. Yes, that could be it. Maybe I was wrong. Maybe I am something else.

What, Ajay? What could you be? You are supposed to be smarter than this. What other beasts drink the blood of people they love? A draugr.

I smell myself.

You don't smell like decay, dummy. Try again, said the voice.

"Okay, voice in my head. What about a fairy? Never mind. I know… I just heard myself.

Maybe I am just human.

The voice asks, *You know any human who drinks blood?*

"Ha, got you, voice in my head; there actually are people like that, so suck it," I say to myself, wondering how much of my mind I have slowly lost in the last few days.

The reality sets in again and, with it, the pain and dismay comes crashing back like a wrecking ball destroying the side of a building, with the debris splattering across the environment. The dreaded emptiness has reeled its way back to me. For a few moments, I forgot the dark space within me. I get up and begin to stumble my way to the next town. Time still remains a haze, but now I walk through the street in search of death. I hunger for my own destruction.

* * *

Hold up again! I call bullshit once again. *Cet enfoiré.* Yes, I said 'this bastard'… He walked to another town. What type of dumb arsehole is he? There is a town of people grieving the death of one of their own right here. They will gladly kill him. I point at Ajay and then at the town. He continues to walk past me and towards the next town. I thought I called time out. I stand watching this unfold.

"Hey, the town is this way," says the narrator.

"Yeah, but you are only here to observe and the story has already taken place. So, this way," says Ajay as he walks towards the next town.

Ajay walks in a state similar to that of a person who has lost all hope and has a lack of any desire. However, this is not entirely true about his desire; it is just directed at something more morbid. Ajay desires death more than anything on this Earth. This path he is on seems destined to bring him closer to the thing he seeks. The reek of decay and death fills the air like a fire consuming all the dead debris around it. The town is in ruins, burnt to the ground many years ago. The fire raged through these streets, killing almost everyone. Ajay walks past what may seem like an old book store. The only building that is still intact. There is an older gentleman in the doorway. Ajay looks at him and the man nods at Ajay.

"That is not possible," says the narrator as he follows Ajay.

"Why?" asks Ajay.

"How did this place in the middle of this charred town survive? This entire town burnt to ground, right?" replies the narrator.

Ajay does not reply to the narrator and just walks past another person. This time, it is a little girl in a bright yellow dress. She seems to be around five or six years old. Ajay smiles at her and she smiles back at him.

He continues on his path, replying to the narrator, "Look again."

When I turn to the little girl, she is still standing there, but now she is blackened by ash. The town is covered in mist and ash that is still falling from the sky. The ruins stand here with the ghosts of the past still lurking in the shadows of this once-sprawling town. As Ajay walks through the ruins of the town, a sign becomes visible in the distance.

'DANGER – KEEP AWAY – MINE AHEAD'.

"Turn around, Ajay," says the narrator.

"Time for you to go. This journey is mine to walk… alone," Ajay says to the narrator.

* * *

You know what needs to be done, says the voice in my head.

"Does not make this any easier," I reply with a heavy heart.

I am surprised at times that a monster like me is still able to feel some emotions, but I can also feel the emptiness. This hollow part of my soul that is expanding at a rapid rate.

We are here, says the voice as I stand looking at the boarded-up entrance.

There are signs all over the place screaming at me. *Stay away!*

The place was abandoned a year before the fire that raged through the town. For this place, it was not enough that people in the town lost their primary source of income. The town was on the verge of death. People lost hope. Hope, the single most important part of human existence. We strive to better our humanity over a simple thing call hope. Once hope dies, the soul soon follows, devouring each part of the light inside all of us. It turns people different shades of dark. The souls that are darkened by this drive to survive begin to take more drastic measures to feel what it is to be alive once more. If only the people of the town did not go down that path. This is what I remember from the story Ria told me.

She said and I quote, "It was horrible; it was so horrible. The mine exploded. People could hear the screams of their fathers and brothers coming from the mine. It was terrifying."

She sobbed when she told me. I always wondered how they could have heard screams. The explosion was caused by a miner hitting a methane pocket that cut off most of the men in the mine. The explosion caused the entire mine to be flooded with carbon dioxide that killed every man in that shaft.

This is the perfect place. I stand here in the middle of the space exactly where the wall caved in. The smell of death remains etched in the air like an obsessive stalker holding on to his beloved. It's as if it has become alive with the souls of the miners. It screams out for more… more souls, more lives so it can grow stronger and more powerful than anything around. The need for lives was so great for death that, a year after the mine disaster, it took the lives of every man, woman and child. Death bled them of life; it ripped their souls from them before charring them to the ground. This place is perfect for my mission. The fall and the sun could not do what it was supposed to, so this landmark for death and destruction will suffice in my hope for death. I take the gun from the bag. I walk towards the centre of the mine where an old chair just sits in the cave. I sit pondering this moment as I stare at the gun and a single tear rolls down my cheek. The drop falls from the end of my chin onto the gun. I know what must be done, but I don't know if I have the courage to do this. The action is very different to that of jumping off a bridge or even waiting to die in the sun's light. I stand up, close my eyes and walk forward. This is a lot harder.

The voice asks, *Is that the gun from Mr Singh's office?*

"It is definitely that gun. We were eighteen when Mr Singh showed Ria and me how to shoot it in the woods. He would say to take off the safety first," I say to the voice as I take off the safety. I continue to explain to the voice in my head, knowing full well that I am explaining this to myself. "I put the gun to my head and pull the trigger. Just that simple. Just that simple."

As if it doesn't know, the voice asks, *Is it loaded?*

I know it is; I made sure of that. The tears begin to flow faster down my face as I hold the gun to my head. Just that simple. Why is this so hard? Why is this moment so hard? I continue to ask myself over and over. I see her. She stands here, staring at me. Her face is not as badly scarred as before. I can see the look in her eyes. The one that says she is concerned about me, as she was many times before.

"You cannot stop this," I say to Ria as I close my eyes and prepare myself for the end. "I am sorry for everything. I am sorry, Ria, but I have to end this."

The echo of the gunshot fills the mine. The bullet shatters and the fragments fall to the dirt on the ground.

"Am I dead?" I ask, too afraid to open my eyes.

There's a smell in the air… I know this smell. This cannot be… I should be dead.

"*I should be dead!*" I yell at the top of my lungs.

The rage begins to take over. I have passed the point of anger. Why has death avoided me? I place the gun to my head once more and begin unloading round after round until all I hear is the clicking of the trigger of an empty gun. I know I should stop, but I just cannot bring myself to. I drop the gun to the floor; it lies there next to the fragments of all the bullets. I am extremely pissed off at this point. I am of two minds. One side of me is horrified at the belief that I am not dead after all of that. I question death. Why has it not taken me? I am in its lair. I stand here awaiting its embrace, but, even here, the palace of its kingdom, I am still alive somewhat. The other side of my mind, the much nerdier side, the side of me that loves Superman comics, just realised that I am bulletproof, but I don't feel like a superhero. I feel anger and hatred for this monster, the vicious monster that I have now become.

I did come prepared. I came prepared if that did not kill me. I have one more trick up my sleeve. I laid dynamite throughout this cave. If I cannot die, this cave of death shall be my tomb. I light the fuse and await my fate.

I am suddenly outside the mine.

"Why?" asks the narrator.

Time is still fuzzy. I fade between timelines.

Kabooooom!

The echo of the blast resonates throughout the town, followed by a violent, heart-wrenching scream vibrating the halls of the cave.

* * *

"He is going to be in there for a while," says the narrator. "For now, we have to be somewhere else — about three towns over. That is right, dear reader, our journey needs to take a slight detour. There is something you need to see."

* * *

There is a person in a hoodie who is partially covered in dirt. The person seems apprehensive, moving at a steady pace. Someone else is here too. They are stalking the person in the hoodie from the bushes. The person nervously mutters as he is startled. "There's nothing there."

He continues to repeat it every few steps. There is a noise from the trees and the hooded man looks at the trees in fright. His face is covered in the shadow of the hoodie, but the glint of his eyes is visible. The man is terrified. The wind blows, but only in the bushes. The nervous hooded man looks at the bushes. He begins to walk faster and then once again a gust of wind blows past the bushes. The man glances at the bushes, but is taken aback by a shadowy figure in the distance. The man backs away and brushes against a tree trunk.

"Don't hurt me," he repeats as he slowly balls up on the ground in fear.

"You okay, man?" asks a man standing near the hooded man.

The man is well dressed in an exquisite three-piece suit. The man seems as if he is of extreme wealth.

"I… I thought you were something else," says the hooded man as the man in the suit holds out his hand to help him up.

With a sigh of relief, the hooded man says, "I was scared for a while there."

"Was? No, my boy, you should still be," says the man in the suit as he pushes the man against the tree trunk.

"Please! No! No!" says the hooded man as the man in the suit reveals his fangs.

"You smell… You smell… delicious," says the hooded man, startling the man in the suit.

"What? Your smell… I can't place it, but it is like you don't have a smell. Why?" asks the man in the suit.

The hooded man looks the man in the suit dead in the eyes as he grabs his hands and breaks his arms. The bones stick out of the skin.

"*Argghhhh!*" screams the man in agony. "What the fuck are you?" he yells as the hooded man removes the hoodie.

It is Ajay. He pulls the man closer to him and whispers, "Now, I don't have to hold back."

Ajay sinks his teeth into the vampire. Blood gushes to the ground as Ajay drains the vampire's life force.

* * *

If you were wondering… This was the night of the explosion in the mine. Ajay found a new purpose, a new mission. He was able to see vampires; they glowed to him. You are now wondering about the larger monster that attacked Ajay. Those… well, I think we have one more stop on this journey before I explain. Now, where were we? That is right. We are now back at the dam. The two soldiers look at each other in shock and awe as they look at Ajay after the bullets have done him no harm.

One of the soldiers says to Ajay, "Those were vampire-killing bullets."

That is where our story is. I will leave Ajay to get back to it.

* * *

Annoyed with the soldiers, I snarled, "Clearly that does not work."

I rifle through my backpack and then throw a round object at the soldiers' feet. The object rolls to a stop in front of a soldier; it is the head of the vampire from earlier.

"That's how you kill a vampire," I say.

The men step back as they look at the head in fear.

"What the fuck are you?" asks a voice from beyond the shadows behind the fence.

"Twice in one night. I'm here to find Alina," I say as I move forward slowly into the sun's rays.

Dawn is now upon us. The sun gleams at me. The shadows of the night are fading away and I can now see the woman in the shadows.

"Alina, I presume," I utter as I continue to move towards the fence.

The soldiers have their weapons locked on me, but hesitate to fire, as they know it is futile.

"You!" she says as she moves towards me.

I stop just twenty-five feet away. I can smell them.

"You should stay there," I warn them.

The hunger is strong. I can try to control it, but barely. I am Ajay. I am not the hunger. My name is Ajay. I am not a monster. I can fight this. Just take a deep breath. But the… sm-smelll… You can hold on…

Alina stares at me for a while as the sun's rays are fully on me. She watches me in amazement, but also fear. I know she is afraid, because I can smell the fear – the soldiers' too.

They smell so deli–

No! I am Ajay! I am not a monster!

Yes, you are, says the voice in my head.

Some Things are Not Pets

I stand in a white room with one very large pane of glass and a mirror to my side. I close my eyes and listen. The silence helps; I can hear them through the glass. There are three – no, four of them in the next room. I hear them, talking about me, about what I am.

"What the hell? Why is that thing not dead? Do you remember what it did to Collens and Andy?" asks one of the voices. His voice sounds older, most likely in his 40s, with a raspy, low voice.

"All of you remember the night we found him," says Alina, or someone I presume to be Alina.

That night… I forgot so much. I remember only bits and pieces of that night, but it is now beginning to become clearer. Time is no longer fuzzy like before. I assume that it was the hunger; it convoluted my storyline. It all makes sense now. I hear them again.

"I remember there was this thing in the sky that we shot down," says another; it sounds like a woman, much younger and with a slight southern accent.

I also remember a bit more about that night. I remember her. I remember the lady vampire. I remember. I remember the monster. I… I… I remember we were flying through the air. I remember someone falling. It was the lady vampire. She fell to the ground as the beast was still feasting on me. I remember it all now.

It held me tight like I was something precious to it, far more precious than any gold or silver. I could feel it draining my soul every second we were in the air. It felt like a dripping bucket, slowly draining away. We were high up in the air when it was struck by a dart or spear. It clutched me tighter as we fell and crashed into a building and, at the time, it was still feeding off me. I could only see its wings as they covered my face. I could hear voices of people nearby, but I was fading fast. I heard it scream; it was a fierce, primal, animalistic bellow.

"Stab it again!" screamed a female voice.

It howled in agony. Its scream echoed through the building and I faded.

* * *

"So what happened to Ajay on that night, you may ask," I ask myself, as the narrator.

From what I can gather, Ajay is pushed aside by the beast and he is on the floor of an open balcony. A group of people have surrounded the beast that lies dying on the floor near Ajay's motionless body. The shrieks continue, but are fading fast. A man from the group walks towards Ajay. The man is in his 40s, had grey hair and a beard, and is around 5-foot-11. He is a military type, with large hands and broad shoulders. He seems like someone who can be the perfect wrestler. He points his gun at him and turns to one of the women – Alina. She is Hispanic, around 5-foot-6, with long black hair and a scar on her right arm that is now covered with a tattoo that states *'Mi mano trae la muerta'*, which translates to 'My hand brings death'. She jabs a large metal spike through the monster's head.

"A, what do I do with him?" asks the man standing above Ajay as he looks at Alina.

"Kill him, Jason," says Alina.

Jason is about to pull the trigger as the sun peeks into the balcony and creeps towards Ajay's hand. Jason points at Ajay's head.

Just as he is about to pull the trigger, Alina yells at him, "*Wait!*"

"What the hell, A?" asks Jason, who seems annoyed.

"Look – the sun," says Alina as she points at Ajay. "He is not burning up – not a vampire."

The sun creeps onto the beast, and its skin bubbles and blisters as it boils in the sun's rays. The skin turns to ash. The flames engulf its body and the beast is now vulnerable to the sun's kiss, and burns in the glory of its embrace. The ashes flutter away into the air, leaving no trace of the beast, but Ajay was still the same, not dead… not yet… and not a vampire that would burst into flames.

"That was that night," says the narrator.

"Not a vampire," repeats Alina.

* * *

Not a vampire. Those words continue to shout out to me.

"Not a vampire," I utter to myself.

The voice asks, *Then what are we?*

I believe it now more than I ever did. The voice in my head, that wretched voice, is a part of me. It is part of my subconscious that continues to keep a shred of the person I was alive. The last part of Ajay's soul. At this point in time, it is right. If I am not a vampire, what am I? Why is my hunger for vampires stronger than my thirst for the blood of others? I ponder this as I stare at the glass pane. I can still hear them in the rooms around me. They are now discussing methods or ways to kill me. Maybe I made a mistake coming here.

Jason says, "We should burn him."

I slowly tap on the window.

Tap… Tap… Tap… Tap…

I stare at him through the glass. I know they can see me and they know I should not be able to see them too. I think I just caught them off guard. I know, right – kinda creepy. I tap the window again and point at the control for the sound system below.

Jason walks over and turns on the mic on my side.

"What?" he asks.

"I've tried that and just about everything you can think of," I say.

"You can hear us? How is that possible? What the hell are you?" asks an older man, who rushes to the window. He is around 5-foot-9; not as buff as Jason.

"What am I? I wish I knew. I can do more than just hear you. I can see all of you. Each one of you has a glow around you and so does every person on this floor and on every floor above us and the two men and three women on the two floors below us," I say to them.

They are startled by the revelation that it is me standing behind this thick glass pane. The younger woman looks terrified. Alina walks to the window and turns on the lights so we are both able to see each other.

"Why are you here?" asks Alina, puzzled by my intention to be here in this… this place – her 'Fortress of Death and Despair' for all vampires.

"I want the thing that made me this way," I reply.

"Enemy of my enemy… Do you thing that makes us friends?" asks Alina.

"I just want to kill those *fucking vampires!*" I say, looking at her.

"What makes you think we would let you go out there?" asks a man standing at the door. He seems like he is in his mid-30s. He is around 6-foot-5 and is built like a tank.

"Simon!" says Jason as he turns to Simon, in slight disagreement with Simon's suggestion.

"Can you see them, smell them? I don't guess if they are a vampire or not. I can also tear them apart. Can you?" I ask as I look directly at Simon.

"What if your hunger takes over and you attack all of us?" asks Jason.

"I understand your caution. I want to know more about the beast and lady vampire and anyway, vampires taste better," I say to Jason.

"How do we trust the monster in you?" asks Jason.

"Lady vampire? Women vampires are very rare; almost impossible that anyone has ever seen one and you have seen one and its second," says Simon.

"What's a second?" I ask curiously.

What are these people talking about female vampires are rare?

"The beast you spoke of before – we call them seconds. With normal vampires, we call them firsts. These are the ones that are more human like – the lures. They lure in the victims and drink their blood and, once they are done, they call in the seconds. These larger monsters are much deadlier than the vampires are. They devour the victim," says Simon.

"No one survives. They never leave any part of the victim. No one survives – no one but you. When we killed the second, it was still feeding. They are vulnerable when they feed. So it is rare to kill one. The general rule is: you hear one, you run," says Alina.

"What have we done?" asks Jason.

* * *

What have you done indeed, you jerk-off, I think as I narrate this story.

I am taking over again. Whatever this is, it's really boring me. So I promised to explain. So here we go.

Vampires cannot turn others into vampires as in the movies. They are born.

The wailing of a baby is heard in the distance. The cries grow louder.

"Can you hear that?" I ask as he looks at the sky.

It seems as if a shooting star is falling to Earth in a fiery blaze, accompanied by a violent, tortured scream as the ball of fire crashes to the ground.

"That is what happens when a vampire is born," I say.

There has been a misconception that vampires have been created from a single blood curse and all vampires were once vampires that were turned by Dracula or something equivalent to a head vampire.

Vampirism is not created; it's in our blood – a simple mutation in the DNA that randomly births a vampire. They are usually males, but there is a rare occurrence when a female vampire is born. When either is born, one of those shooting stars falls to the ground. You have heard of guardian angels, right. We all have one; they are born to each one of us and they are there to guide and protect us, but, for vampires, it is different. The guardian angels that are assigned to vampires go through a transformation that sends them crashing and burning to the Earth. The fallen angels' purpose is to protect their wards, but the rules are different between male and female vampires. Male vampire seconds usually stay further away than with female vampires; this is due to their rarity. This does not mean that female vampires are weaker; far from it – they are stronger and faster than their male counterparts are. For those of you who think that a female and male vampire can create vampires by procreation… well, no, not possible. Unfortunately, I do not have that information. There are not many female vampires lurking around stalking young men in the darkness (insert weird laughter from the narrator – slaps forehead).

Anyway. The main purpose of a second is to kill those on whom a vampire feeds. In ancient times, vampires that were lords with castles and land would leave the heads of those they fed on as a warning to anyone who opposed them. Grotesque is more what I would call it. I have had my share of… moments, but that is a different story.

Vampires – that's where we are. Vampires feed off blood plasma and the seconds devour the person's soul and body. So what happens when the victim survives? Simple: we end up with Ajay, more like a vampire terminator (slaps forehead again). Yeah, I know – *merde!* I know that was dumb. The victim turns into a vicious vampire-feasting beast that is able to kill a vampire. You can call it karma.

What goes around comes back to bite you in the arse. Okay, not the arse, but you get what I mean. Funny and ironic. The vampire's meal goes through a change and becomes the thing that will feast on the vampire. There are still some things even I do not know yet.

Here ends the lesson on these worthless beings. There he is again. Ajay is in the sun's rays staring at the horizon. A vampire killer. Yet these humans think they can keep him like some fucking pet. If only he knew six months ago that his life would go down this path, but such is life. Now the hunted will hunt the hunters in search of hope that out there somewhere is the one thing that can change him back to Ajay – the Ajay before all of this. The years have passed. I will let him tell you where we are, but, for that, we are going to jump around the timeline a bit.

* * *

This voice… I remember this voice in my head. It is as if I have been losing this part of me the more the darkness has been taking over. Every time I become this thing, I slowly begin to change – change; is that the right word? I wish I could call this an evolution, but, dear voice in my head, what am I evolving into? That's the problem; this is not an evolution – it's more like a metamorphosis into something I should be terrified of. That growl – do you hear it? Do you hear it, voice in my head, or was it just my imagination? Voice in my head, you are my imagination too. What if the growls are the darkness creeping forward? What if it is the reason I have not spoken to you in a while, because I now fear that Ajay is no more? I fear that Ajay has now transformed into this beast, this hungry, vile, self-preserving monster. I hear it again. The howl of the wind is growing louder. Voice, are you still there? I hope so. Voice, I see someone. Voice… There is only silence now, but you are standing here. I see you, shadowy figure. The howling of the winds grows. I can see you. Is it real or my imagination?

Ria stands in front of me in the exact clothes she wore that night – you remember that night I killed her. That night, the hunger was too strong for me. She stares at the monster before her. I remain unfazed by the sight of her. The beast I have become has finally taken over my mind. This new manifestation before me may be the last hope of humanity I conjured into the only thing in the entire world I loved more in my life. A reminder… No, a warning to the Ajay I once was that, no matter how long I live, I will never go back to the version of me that once was. I have one purpose at this point in time: kill the thing that made me this way. Like in all those books and movies, I will hopefully return to my human side. However, I realise that I will never be able to escape the truth – the same truth that stands here before me. The one that still just stares at me as she did many times before. Before, when she wanted to say something to me, Ria's lips moved slowly.

"Let the pain go, Ajay," says Ria, her words echoing through the room, reverberating through every part of this building.

"I wish I could," I reply as I drop to my knees. "I wish I could."

The wind stops howling and, with it, she vanishes. A gust of wind blows past me once more, but this time it feels different. That smell. I know that smell.

The darkness is calling to me. I feel it clawing at me. I feel the monster. I feel his sinister darkness.

I get back to my feet.

"Forgot about you," I say as I search the rafters intensely.

Another gust of wind blows past me and then, in succession, a few more gusts of wind blow past. Intimidation? Haha.

"Vampire One, Vampire Two and Vampire Three, you boys really want to play like this?" I ask.

"Abomination! How do you see us?" asks Vampire Two as the three become visible.

I stand in silence as the trio begins to circle me. I am trapped.

"Nothing to say, half-breed!" shouts Vampire Three as he fake-lunges at me.

I remain calm and unshaken by this bunch of halfwits. I have seen this type of dummy my whole life; just a bunch of bullies. I stare at the wall and pay no attention to them. They continue to circle me like vultures circling a dying carcass.

Vampire One lunges forward, trying to grab me, but, as he moves forward, I vanish and he crashes into Vampire Two.

"Dimwit!" yells Vampire Two as he pushes Vampire One off him.

The trio begins to search the room for me.

A shadowy figure appears at the end of the hallway. The trio walks towards it. As they move closer, they see it's… me. I am facing away from the trio. Vampire Two grabs my right shoulder.

"Got you now, abomination," says an overconfident Vampire Two.

"Time to end this," says Vampire One, revealing his fangs before violently biting into my left shoulder.

Vampire Two and Vampire Three also bite me. Vampire Two has me on the right shoulder and Vampire Three is biting into my neck. I remain motionless as the trio feast on my blood. Vampire Three is the first to pull himself away. He stares at me with a disgusted expression. I stand here with a sinister smile. A smile that is right. It is as if I want them to… as if I made them pawns in my game of chess that I strategically set up with every move accounted for.

Vampire Three begins to groan in pain as he falls to the fall, disturbing Vampire One and Vampire Two.

"Vampire Three!" exclaims Vampire Two.

"What the hell have you done?" demands Vampire One as he focuses on me.

Vampire Two is the next. He begins to groan and then Vampire One too. The two fall to the floor in tandem exactly where they stood, cocky and so sure that this was my end.

I take a step towards Vampire Three.

"Hurts, does it not?" I ask as I walk closer and closer.

I stalk him, but I am interrupted by a gust of wind. This one is different; the smell is different. Lavender… I smell lavender.

I turn to the end of the hall and there is another shadowy figure.

"This is going to be a bit messy," I say to the figure.

I turn to the three vampires, revealing my fangs before I vanish before them.

* * *

The moonlit night is riddled with the echoes of the trio's screams. I know, dear reader. I need to take over at this point. The gruesomeness of the deaths are too much, even for someone like me. I don't think you are ready to see him like this… not just yet.

Ajay bursts through the door of the building. He is drenched in blood that covers every part of him. He stares at the moon with a very distant expression. The thing he was searching for was not found. The continuous search has driven him further down a rabbit hole from which he may not be able to claw his way out. The darkness within him is now matured to a new level. The Ajay from before is now dead. The battle within is lost, but… but seeing Ria… maybe, just maybe there is some form of hope left. Maybe her presence is the last bit of Ajay that is still alive deep within his core. That is what Ajay hopes is true. Ajay is still staring at the full moon and, as he basks in is light, he is startled by multiple presences that he can feel coming over the horizon. Their echoes are resonating through the air. He has sensed this before. There are three of them. He can hear their sonar echo. They call for their wards.

"I gotta get the hell out of here," whispers Ajay as he turns to flee the area as fast as he can.

The echoes are getting louder. As Ajay tries to leave, he is brought to his knees in pain. He has felt this as well. It is as if his skin is burning from inside and out. He tries to hold back his screams of agony, but it hurts so much; the pain is too much. He looks at the skin on his arms as he rips off his shirt sleeves. His arms are rapidly changing colour from his normal skin colour to a pale white. His skin is as white as snow and becomes thicker and firmer. This has never happened to him before. The sonar echo is louder now and Ajay can hear the beasts' whispers and screeches – three seconds.

Ajay remembers what Alina once told him and those words echo.

When you hear a second, you run. Those mother– Those things will rip you apart. They are near indestructible. There is a way to kill one, but only when they are feeding. That is when they are vulnerable.

Ajay tries to drag himself away from the echoes of death. He may be indestructible too, but he has never gone up against a guardian angel, let alone fallen angels with a soul thirst. He claws into the dirt as much as he can; he pulls himself up with intense pain. The pain grows stronger with each passing moment. He is fighting as much as he can. The echoes are louder now. They sound as if a bell is being tolled right near his head. He feels them. They are here. It is too late. It is too late. How can this be? His mission cannot end, not like this. Ajay turns towards them. He covers his face. The seconds are here. They are grotesque monsters. They are pitch-black, which make some sense, as they were burnt in the fall to Earth. The have elongated fingers with large nails. They have wings like a bird, with feathers. Their eyes are red, with no pupils. They have hair as well, but each has a different style. One has long hair, while the other two have short hair. They have long, pointed noses and distorted cat-like facial features. They look at Ajay. He is in serious trouble now.

The pain is too much for him and he lets out a monstrous scream that echoes in the area. It startles the seconds, which begin to move towards him, but they are halted by a gale-force wind that blows towards the seconds, but to no other place. The wind's force intensifies as it pushes the seconds back. Ajay, still in pain, turns to his right and there she is.

"Heyyy," says Ria as she gazes into Ajay's eyes.

It is like the day she first told him that she loved him. He starts to scream in pain once more. The agony is too intense and, with just a simple touch on his forehead, Ria is able to render him unconscious.

"I got you," she whispers to him.

She loves him. Why else would she have given up eternity in Paradise just to come back as a spirit haunting the Earth? Haunting him. No, not haunting him. She is his protector. She will always be his protector. His love. His world. Heaven cannot stop her from being with him. Neither can those monsters. He is hers and she is his.

The wind intensifies once more and is now at a speed equivalent to a hurricane. The seconds are pushed back further, but are fighting back.

Ria takes her attention from Ajay and places her focus on the seconds. She goes from concerned to rage-fuelled monster.

"*You can't have him!*" Ria yelled at the seconds.

The wind dies down. The seconds now have a chance to attack Ajay; they charge forward, rushing in at bullet train speed.

Slam!

The long-haired second is slammed with a tree that was ripped out of the ground by the roots, with soil still surrounding the roots. The two remaining seconds now focus their attention on Ria. They did not take her seriously before, but now… now, they do. She is a threat, one that needs to be stopped at any cost. Ajay can wait; he is not going anywhere. They lunge towards her. The air around Ria becomes violent and blows towards the seconds, pushing them further back, but they are relentless and continue to fight forward. They inch forward. They are getting closer and closer. Ria is trying to force them back, but they get up and push forward again. Ria, enraged, bellows an earth-shaking, glass-shattering and ear-piercing scream that brings the two seconds to their knees. They are writhing in pain. Their screams go unheard, blocked out by Ria's scream. In an instant, as she has them fallen to the ground, Ria is seized by the long-haired second. He clasps her from behind.

All she can think is, *How is this possible?*

The second wastes no time, as he knows how dangerous she is, and he bites her neck. Ria truly cannot catch a break – bitten twice. The remaining seconds begin to rise slowly, still tortured by the pain. Ria can feel her life force begin to fade. She begins to violently shake and vibrate. In the blink of an eye, Ria vanishes. Ajay looks around cautiously in search of her. The other two begin to search for her too. They slowly move closer to the long-haired second. He begins to twitch; his hands begin to tremble uncontrollably. He tries to scream, but cannot move his mouth. The trembles move to the rest of his body, which is now shaking violently. It is as if he is having a seizure and, just as fast as it started, it stops, as if nothing happened. The others look at the long-haired second in fear.

Splat!

With tremendous force, the long-haired second explodes, pieces scattering all over the night sky. The area is covered in a mist of blood particles that have scattered everywhere. There she stands, right there in the place the long-haired second stood before. She phased into the second and used the molecules in his body to destroy him. The remaining seconds are not shaken by the death of one of their own; they continue to rush towards Ria. They grab her forcefully and drag her to the ground. Each of the seconds sinks its teeth into her. Their bites are much different from the vampires. Their jaws dislocate and two sets of fangs are visible from both ends of their mouths. Ria can feel the essence of her soul begin to drain as the seconds feed off her. They continue to bleed her soul, but remain unaware of a figure standing in the misty, blood-filled air. Ria now feels like she is in more trouble. The long-haired second has returned, but how can this be possible? No… There is something different about that shadow; it is much larger than the others and has larger wings.

The monster moves closer. The two seconds are aware of the humongous beast that approaches them. The monster grabs one of the two seconds by its head. The beast's hand wraps around the second's head and encloses it as if it was a small marble clutched in the hands of a grown man. The beast looks at the other second and then vanishes into the mist with the second in its hand. The other second lets go of Ria and tries to flee, but is unable to, as it cannot move. Ria controls the air around it and forces it to the ground. In a flash, the last second is ripped away by the larger beast.

Ria stands there in the sea of red mist. She is trying to comprehend why the beast is trying to kill its own kind. Ajay… She almost forgot about Ajay. She turns to where he was before, but only sand and grass are there. She looks around, but now she also knows she has one thing to do: prepare for battle once more. Whatever that thing is, it is there in the mist and now she can see the outlines of its silhouette. She is not afraid, though she should be; that beast just ripped apart two seconds as if they were nothing.

The seconds are said to be indestructible, but not for that beast; they were like toys that he just flung around. As I said before, she is not scared of it. It feels familiar to her. There is something about the beast that reminds her, as she whispers, "Ajay."

It walks closer, but is still hidden in the mist. It is 8-foot tall with wings opened and around 10 feet or more across. It has a much scarier look than the normal second does. There is no hair on its body, and it has curved, claw-like fingers. Its skin is greyish-white and it has a smaller nose and long jawline, but its eyes are red, with sapphire-blue pupils. It looks nothing like Ajay, but she can feel his presence.

It spreads its wings and then rockets into the sky, vanishing into the mist and the night. Ria looks as the beast takes off and then she vanishes into the night as well, leaving only blood, death and despair filling a night that was once peaceful and bare.

CHAPTER FIVE

Something About the Need to Survive

I stand here, 47 years later, in front of my own gravestone. Next to me is my mother's gravestone.

"I never got to say how sorry I was for leaving. I never got to tell her how much I loved her and how much it hurt to not be there like a son should have been. I failed in every way. I failed her and I failed you," I say as I stare at the gravestones before turning to Ria, who stands behind me.

"I have told you to let it go, but I understand, Ajay," says Ria as she walks towards me. She places her hand on my shoulder.

I can smell her. It is her smell – lavender.

"You are real," I say to her with the last bit of humanity that remains, the tears flowing down my cheeks.

"Kind of," she replies.

"What does kind of mean?" I ask before she fades away.

"Hmmmm."

I just stand here surrounded by death. The past lies below my feet as I walk through the cemetery. I feel as if I am being watched from the shadows around me, but I can also feel something else – this one has a more familiar presence and it's further away… Never mind. Dear voice, its gone; might have been nothing.

You know it's not, but it may be back, says the voice.

"So you are back; been a long while, voice in my head," I say to myself. Not weird at all.

* * *

I stand here – another familiar place. The chain-link fence; the dam. So many memories, so many friends, and a few enemies too. I find myself following a path that has returned me to the past.

"Je suis revenue,"[1] I whisper.

I know they are watching. Much has changed since my last time here. They used guards at the gates, but now, as I look at the sky… Now, they have a much more dangerous guard.

---

1 "I have returned."

He is up there, well beyond the clouds. He knows I am here and he should still remember what I am. I walk forward to the gates as I did all those years ago.

The elevator doors open slowly. I can sense them behind the door; three of them with weapons pointed at me. I take it they have never heard of me; well, that is obvious, as I have not been here since that night. They point their weapons at me as the doors open and I just stand there staring at the level of stupidity before me. I mean, if the guard above was not brave enough to take me on, what makes them think they can with those weapons? I move slowly as two more come out of the corridor and they have weapons too. Great – unnecessary deaths. I raise my hands to signal my surrender. Four more with weapons join the team before me.

"Nice welcome," I whisper.

"*Je suis revenue…*" I have returned. "Been a long time, Ajay," says a familiar voice from the past. This one is not Alina. The voice has a French accent.

"*Bonjour,* Renée; it's been a minute, kid," I say as she walks out of the darkness and into the light.

She reminds me of Alina and our very first encounter. Renée is around 64 years old, with white hair tied in a single ponytail that hangs down her chest. She has no weapons on her.

I continue, "Nice welcome; you have six more behind me and eight more around the left side."

"More than forty years for you to return," says Renée as she motions for everyone to lower their weapons.

"Someone still remembers me," I say as I look at the sky and salute the winged man above the clouds.

"You seem different, a lot less fearful of the hunger," says Renée as I walk towards her.

"I am still hungry, but, by the smell here, you are definitely not on the menu," I say as I move closer to her with eyes following my every move.

"What is on the menu?" asks Renée with a fearless expression.

"Vampires and guardians; they taste better." I laugh and then turn serious again. "Word is you know something that hunts and kills them."

We walk into the facility and down a dark passage. Renée leads us to the end of the corridor. She closes the door.

"There is a lore – it was ancient, something from very long before. The lore was about a beast that was created for the sole purpose of hunting vampires and all its kind. This beast," she says as she rummages through piles of books and papers scattered everywhere. "This beast was… uhm… was designed and made by a man; one man in particular. Right, here it is." She finds an old scroll.

I stay a distance away. My bloodlust is controlled, but I will not risk it.

"His name was Xerxes. He did an experiment on himself – a sort of blood transfusion. He mixed the blood of vampires, guardians and different variations of wolves," she says.

I stop her. She stares at me in slight confusion.

"You mean he created a werewolf," I utter.

"Yes, but this was just lore. I don't know if it was possible to create such a creature!" she exclaims.

"It is possible – and much more than that, it is real," I say.

Her confusion turns to intrigue. "No, cannot be. This person would not be able to survive a procedure such as this," says Renée.

"Explain that to Andrew," I say.

"Andrew?" She looks at me, confused.

"The bird man above in the sky," I say.

"That's different. What you are talking about is a creature that can change into a wolf on a moonlit night," says Renée.

She is interrupted by sirens at the dam facility.

"What the hell could that be?" asks Renée as she rushes to her communication device.

"That, my dear, is the werewolf," I say to her as I turn to the door.

She looks afraid; that is new. I have not seen her afraid before.

I look at her and continue, "He is here for me. Only me."

* * *

"I definitely was," says the narrator. "Now for my official introduction. Hello, I am Alexandre, or just Alex, and I am… Well, dear reader, you have a guessed it by now. I'm the werewolf."

* * *

Something large begins to slam on the door. It snarls and a howl is heard throughout the corridor. It is the howl of an angry, vicious animal prepared to rip a person to shreds.

The howls echo in the night; the screams terrify my mind. I hear it repeatedly in fright. How I fear the horrors of the wolf that lurks at night.

* * *

A howl is heard beyond the door before the door explodes open with a powerful blow from the werewolf. Talk about convenient timing; this wolf has very perfect timing. We just spoke about him and here this motherfu– Here he is and he is ready to kill me. His glowing yellow eyes glare at me. My, my, Mr Wolf, what big teeth you have. Let's see if you can do what others have failed to do. He steps forward with purpose; that purpose is me. He is around 7-foot-5 tall. His fur is a mix of black and brown shades. Did I mention the yellow glowing eyes? At this moment, I have completely forgotten about Renée. I see him. All I see is him; this daunting presence that is right before me. He stares at me and then he rushes towards me in the blink of an eye, with his claws out, ready to rip me to bits, but he misses as I move just enough to escape him. He grunts and then turns towards me.

"Why do you not want to die?" asks the werewolf as he shows his paws with huge, sharp claws.

"You speak." I am genuinely amazed. "You have come a long way, my friend," I say to him as I walk towards the exit.

"Don't call me that! *Putain de fils de pute!*[2] yells the werewolf.

"*Ce n'est pas gentil,*[3] you overgrown fucking lapdog!" I reply.

In an instant, he vanishes before me.

---

2 "Fucking son of a bitch!"

3 "That's not nice."

Slam!

He grabs me and pushes me to the wall. His hands are massive and he grips me as if I am a rag doll. You know, like when King Kong grabs the lady. Okay, so that is somewhat of an exaggeration, but you get the idea. He comes closer to me.

"I end you tonight for what you did to me," he says – or something to that effect.

I cannot pay attention. I just cannot focus. That smell… The hunger is getting stronger. I can smell…

I smell…

"We smell vampire!" says the voice.

"Yes, we do," I say as the vampiric hunger heightens.

I… am… losing… control.

"We smell vampire!" repeats the voice.

Yes, I know, but from where…?

"No, not from where. It's from were… wolf," says the voice.

I can feel my blood boiling. I have felt this before. Earlier… Yes, I remember the werewolf is about to bite me. His mouth opens wide and he moves closer to me. I am in deep trouble. What do I do now?

I kick him clear across the room. I am no longer myself. I have not been myself for a very long time, but you know what I mean. The lust for blood has taken over my body and the last bit of my mind. I transform into a version of me that is terrifying. This version of me is a hairless, seven-foot winged beast that now stands before the werewolf. It only sees the blood of the vampire that is within the beast. I hunger for that blood. I rush towards the werewolf, but, in an instant, I am caught in a vortex of wind. I try to move, but cannot. The werewolf rises and charges towards me, but he, too, has been ensnared in a vortex of his own. We stare at each other – me with hunger and him with hatred and rage. That smell… lavender. I smell her. Ria appears before both of us. The vortex begins to become a vacuum. I cannot breathe, but I see him fading too. I can't… I… I… I… I…

* * *

I awaken to find myself in a familiar setting. I am in the basement at the dam facility. The place looks different. The paint still smells fresh. As I lock up, I see many glows of people above. I know these silhouettes. I am back here at the facility forty-seven years ago. It has been more than a year since the day I joined this group of vampire exterminators. Most of them still fear me. I remain at a distance from them. The hunger is too strong. I wish I could control it around them, but they smell so…

Stop, yells the voice.

It still keeps me in check. I am still Ajay and not the monster. I know, I know. This journey has been arduous every minute in this basement. I can see them all, just walking around the bunker. For many, I am a myth that remains below. You know, like an urban legend that no person has seen, but everyone has heard of. I am the boogeyman under the bed. The bunker is full of lives, souls with blood… Blood… No, no… Those are families up there. Those are mothers, fathers, sons, daughters, sisters and brothers. You remember what a family is, right?

How I miss you. How I wish I could be there with my mother, Ria, her parents, my family.

I would destroy this world to get back all of that. I would give up this immortality for just a moment with them. If I– When I find the vampire that bit me and kill her, all of this goes back to normal. I get back to normal. Normal… I wish I knew what that feels like. It looks as if Alina is on her way down to my space in hell. I can see her in the room next to me. She seems different in a way. She is about to get onto the comms, but she is hesitant. I have not seen her in this light. Something is up and she is way too anxious.

"Ajay."

I hear her voice over the comms and even her tone seems off.

"Ajay, we found a place with a mass of vampires all at the same time," says Alina.

"That's good, right?" I reply. I can only think of all that blood.

"No. On any normal day, I would say this is going to be a walk in the park, but we have two very dangerous problems. There are two seconds protecting the place, but this is all we can see now. With the number of vampires there, we are surely going to run into more," says Alina in a concerned tone.

I look at her through the two-way mirror. She is right to be concerned. We will be walking into unknown territory. I weigh in on the difficulty that we may run into, but also the bloodlust is making it harder to just let this one go. I have not eaten in a while.

"Hell, hon. I am hungry for vampire. How about you?" I ask her as I let go of any feelings I have of the danger we are going to be in.

She pauses for a moment as she stares at me.

"Get ready; we have bloodsuckers to exterminate," she commands.

I see the tension and concern she had has now past. No more anxiety. She is reborn by the hatred we share of these vile creatures.

I look at the levels above and witness the dedication of the soldiers above as they arm themselves for the impending massacre. I walk down the corridor to the war room. You know, a place where people plan for war. Enter shrug here… Haha. Well, at least your humour is still weak.

As I walk to the war room, I am reminded of the hatred I have for those vampires. Why would I not hate them? They have taken everything from me. That one… She stole my life, my future with Ria. Ria! Is that price worth more than just her death? I want suffering, pain, anguish, torture and a violent slow death for that lady vampire, but that would not even be worth the price of what I lost.

I stand by the doorway. I stand much further back. The smell in the war room makes me fear the hunger will take over and I will return to a monster.

I listen in on the briefing, but my mind keeps taking me to the night and that woman. I pray for one thing and one thing only – that she is there and I get to her first.

I can see Jason and Alina walking around the room. They are talking about the location and entry into the place.

"The nest is in an abandoned building in an outer section of a small town," Jason says as I fade out, still watching each person present their ideas for an attack plan.

My mind. My mind is focussed on ripping apart that vampire *bitch*.

"That won't work," says a voice from a few feet behind me.

"What?" asks Jason as he looks at me.

I shrug at him as if to say 'dude, not me'.

A young woman walks towards the war room. I can smell her. I am trying desperately to not attack her, but this one has always been much braver than the others. She smiles at me as she walks. I smile back, but all I can think of is pizza. She smells like a tasty slice of pizza. I love pizza – so did Ria. I hold it together as much as I can.

"You were saying, Renée," says Alina.

Renée is a bright young woman. We spend a lot of time playing chess and reading books, but this is the first time I have been this close to her.

"All of this won't work. You have forgotten about the fact that, once we kill the first vampire, its second will race towards us," says Renée.

"Then what do we do?" asks Jason.

"What about the plan you had?" asks Renée as she looks at me.

Alina looks at me. "Do you believe it will work?"

I nod at her.

"What? What will work?" asks Jason as the entire room of people stare at the monster among them.

They all turn back to each other and walk through the plan with Renée. I feel a breeze – how is it possible? All the way down here, a breeze. There is a smell – lavender. The smell is coming from the long, dark passage.

"Don't," says the voice.

I know I should not. I know that this is a very bad idea, but I also know that smell and the memories that come with that smell. The memories begin to rush through my mind with flashes of images, and every single one is her. Every single moment is a moment of Ria. Ria on the porch that night. Ria when she clocked Dickhead. Mark – that was his name. Ria under the bridge. Ria when we walked home every day. Ria the first day we met. I am here at the end of the corridor. The smell is stronger here, but there is no one here. I turn back to the war room and, as I walk back to the doorway, I swear I can feel someone or something watch me. I stop. I know you are here; maybe it's not yet time. The smell of lavender vanishes.

* * *

Night falls at an old building. It looks like it was once a manor or mansion for the elite who live in the city. There is a fleet of vehicles parked on the grass. The vehicles range from exotic to weird, like there is a hearse here and an ambulance.

The estate is far away from any form of civilisation. The air is silent, much like the estate itself. There is no movement on the ground and no guards outside. There two guards walking rotation inside a hallway near a staircase. There is a knock at the door.

"I'll check it out," says one of the men.

There is a knock at the door once again. The guard gets to the door before another knock comes. He unlocks the door and opens it to me standing here.

"What do you want?" he asks in a hostile tone as he looks at me with anger, but the anger turns to confusion as he continues to stare at me, confused by what stands before him.

The evil intentions and hunger are raging inside me.

"What are you?" he gasps.

I grab him by the neck and pull him through the doorway onto the gravel driveway some 20 feet away. He lands hard and is surrounded by five vampire hunters geared up in tactical clothing and with guns pointed at his head.

"What are you?" he utters.

"Vampire killers. Make my day," says Jason. He is kind of a huge *Dirty Harry* fan.

"Humans… Why can I not smell you?" asks the vampire.

The vampire is strapped up and gagged. The hunters place him in the back of a truck. I enter the building alone. I can see the other vampire guard near the staircase.

As he moves to the first step of the staircase, he calls out, "What was it?"

There is silence in the hallway and this concerns the guard.

"Simon!" he exclaims as he turns to the doorway.

I grab him, squeeze his neck and raise him off the ground just a bit. He is a bit taller than I am. Okay, he is a lot taller than I am. The hunger is raging inside and I can feel it taking its toll on my soul. I can smell him. I just want to…

No, Ajay, says the voice.

I tighten my grip on the vampire's neck. The hunger is getting stronger. I move closer to him. I can smell him. I can see his lips move.

"Freak!"

I stare him dead in the eyes. I can see the fear. Just one bite; it won't hurt anyone except him. I starve for blood. I starve so much for blood. I pull in closer and I am ready to bite his neck when I hear a voice.

"Ajay!"

This voice is not in my head. It is Jason. I squeeze the guard's neck just enough to render him unconscious. He remains alive; that can't be right… Awake… No, no… He breathes.

"You good?" asks Jason as I turn to him.

"I'm good," I reply as I walk to the staircase.

"Talk to me, Ajay," says Alina as I close my eyes and feel the area.

"There are floors below us and it also seems like a cave system below. Three floors below us, there are around 100 vampires gathered there. I can see them. I can see something else below – it has a different glow to it. It must be a guardian. It is moving, sort of. I think it's feeding. We have time to take out as many as we can before that thing alerts the other seconds," I say.

"Then let's move," says Jason and he soldiers on.

"Two of your guys are almost at their position. Just about ten seconds," I say.

"How can you see us?" asks a curious Jason.

"I'm not them," I reply and then look at Alina. "Time to go to work."

Jason commands over the walkie-talkies, "Go time!"

I can see some worry and fear in Jason as we reach the third level. I can see it; Alina was never fearful of me like Jason is. She took a massive chance on me; she didn't have to. She could have let me die a long time ago.

"What are you going to do?" asks Jason.

"I'll take the room at the end of the hall; there are about thirty of them there. Might be fun," I say.

As I step forward, I feel a presence that stops me.

"Ajay?" asks Alina.

"There's something in that room," I say.

"What is it?" asks Alina.

I just shake my head.

"We will come with you," she says.

If you are squeamish, you may want to read with caution.

The doors open to more than fifty vampires in a single room. Most are in lab coats. They seem to be doctors or something. They all turn towards us. I look at them, the hunger and bloodlust taking over. It screams at me. It wants me to bleed these fucking things dry.

"I am trying to control it, Alina," I say as the vampires walk towards, confused about what we are.

I see several guards move towards us, but it feels like time has slowed. None of them expected us to be down here.

I turn to Alina. I look at her in a way to ask for permission. Permission to make them *fear* me.

"Well, let it out," she commands.

I turn to the vampires with a smile that has a hint of malice and menace behind it.

I lunge forward. Jason and Alina begin to fire rounds of vampire-killing bullets into the crowd. I can hear bullets in the rooms around us as well. The massacre has begun. The guards rush towards me. One of the guards pounces on me with his fangs out and he is prepared to bite me, but I grab his jaw as it nears my face. I can smell his overconfidence dissipate and change to fear as I squeeze his jaw. I look at his fangs and then his eyes.

"Mine are bigger," I cockily utter as I sink my fangs into his neck and break his jaw, with blood streaming to the floor.

I scream with a primal, feral rage. My fingers are now longer, with extended fingernails. I turn to the other vampires. I see their fear turn to terror.

"This cannot be," says a man in a coat, but I pay no attention.

The bloodlust has taken over and I rush forward, clawing my way through each vampire in front of me. I use my claws and ram them directly into the skull of a vampire and, using my other hand, I hold his body while biting it. One by one, I rip through the vampires. Blood flows throughout the room. Pieces of matter and brains drip from my hand like jelly. I make my way through the horde, but I am now aware of my surroundings. The bloodlust is strong, but not as strong as before. This rooms looks like a lab of sorts. Oops… I just used a Bunsen burner to char the face of another guard. It smells like a Sunday roast – well, that is what it smells like for me. I use both my hands as a stake and push through the monster's body and blood gushes. I rip his body in two and take a minute to watch the blood, heart, lungs and guts spill onto the floor. Man, this is fun. I look around and it seems as if that was the last one. Well, that sucks. As I walk to Jason, he just stares at me.

"Do I have something in my teeth?" I ask as Alina walks towards us.

Jason just stands there. At this point, I am not sure if he is in shock or just in awe.

"Look down," says Alina.

I look at myself. I am covered in blood and bits of vampire.

"Sorry, I never was such a messy eater," I say as I sense the thing from earlier.

It is faint, but there is a glow.

"Hey, A! There is something behind this door," I say to Alina.

Jason and Alina raise their weapons as we walk towards the door. I open the door and we walk into another operating-type room. There is a gurney in the middle of the room. There is also a large table to the left of the room. The room reminds me of a meat factory in a way. It has those plastic curtains hanging around the operating table. There is some sort of yellow substance patched on the floor. Alina walks to the table. The table is covered with piles of books and scattered papers. The books look ancient. There are a few scrolls lying around as well. Alina picks up a book titled *Evolution of Species* by Dr X Martin. She flips through the book while I look at the plans on the table. These plans are not building plans – these are odd. They are plans for a winged man. I cannot make out the words on the plans – it is in Latin – but one word is ringed with a highlighter and marked 'donor'.

Jason scans the outer end of the room.

"Lina!" exclaims Jason.

Alina and I rush over through the plastic curtains and there he is chained and hoisted onto the wall like a prize – a naked man on the wall, but he is different, altered. He has long wings with claws at the ends of his wings.

"Are those wings and feathers?" asks a stunned Alina.

Jason moves closer to the winged man. "Looks like it."

"What the hell are these vampires making down here?" asks Alina as she walks closer to the young man.

Jason points at the book Alina has. "The evolution to our species."

Jason points his weapon at the winged man.

"Is he a vampire?" asks Renée from the back of the room.

I turn to Renée. "No, I do not smell vampire in him. He may still be human, barely, but still human," I say.

Alina goes to touch the winged man. As she places her hand on his wing, he moves. She shuffles back. Jason is ready to shoot.

"We have to kill it!" yells Jason.

Alina is fearful; I can sense it as she nods in affirmation.

Jason prepares to kill the young man when I feel a hand on my shoulder. It startles me. It must be Renée. No, none of them are brave enough to touch me, but she did walk past me in the bunker. I know this hand. I know that smell — lavender. I turn cautiously to the being next to me. I look at the hand and slowly look at her neck; it is scarred with two bite marks on her right side. Ria! She is in tears; her scarred face is in tears. She does seem less scarred than the last time she popped up. I can see more of her face. I can see more of my Ria. She is focussed on the winged man. She peers deep within my soul.

"I know… I know, Ria," I say to her as she vanishes.

"*Stop!*" I yell.

"What the hell?" questions Jason.

"We need all the help we can get to destroy these monsters," I say as I look at the young man.

"Fuck," utters Jason.

Alina asks, "You sure?"

I nod at her as I go closer to the winged man and help to unchain him. Is this place hotter than normal? I shuffle my shirt collar; it is getting hotter. I feel a fierce burning sensation. I feel like my blood within me is on fire. It's like when you see boiling water bubble and turn to steam. I can see some sort of vapour around my hand. I fall to my knees in agony. I scream so loudly that the echo vibrates the walls. Imagine an earth tremor that lasts for a few seconds.

"Ajay!" screams Renée as she rushes to me.

I try to scan the area, still writhing in pain.

"Guardian… Guardian not… not feeding anymore," I barely manage to utter before crashing to the floor.

"Get him out," says Alina to Renée, and she then looks at Jason. "Get them both out of here now."

Alina grabs a bunch of explosives and races to the staircase.

Jason and two other soldiers grab the winged man. He opens his eyes, regaining consciousness.

"Release me," he says to the men.

"You are safe. We got you," I say to him as he turns to me.

His grimace turns into a smile of sorts. Renée has me. She is slightly shorter than I am and she is here as my crutch. For once, the hunger is not the thing that scares me. This pain is all my body can think about; it is driving the hunger and bloodlust to be pushed down. I know Renée is right below my arm. I can smell her, smell her blood, but it does not matter at this moment. The pain is excruciating. I try desperately to suppress it. Just a few feet and I can get to the outside. I move with her, one step at a time. One foot forward, next foot forward. Alina is near the staircase and we are far behind. The winged man looks at me and nods as if he understands that he is now safe.

"What's your name?" I ask him as I look at him and then at the floor, trying to scan the floors below for the guardian.

"Andrew. My name is Andrew," says Andrew.

"Nice to meet you, Andrew. I am Ajay," I say.

"You are different. Did they make you too?" asks Andrew.

"Something like that," I say to him as my attention goes to Renée. "Renée, I need you to shout for Alina. It's– Argh! In the bell tower," I manage to say.

"*Alina! Bell tower!*" yells Renée as she points at the ceiling.

Alina understood immediately. Her mission has now become more dangerous. The guardian is awake, not feeding.

Alina nods t Renée. "Get them out."

The ceiling and the walls vibrate violently; it feels like an earthquake at magnitude three. As we walk, the vibration intensifies to an earthquake of magnitude six. Alina is on the staircase; I can see her… well, barely.

My blood and insides feel like they are being boiled by extreme heat. I fall to the floor screaming. I cannot comprehend the level of pain I am experiencing. Renée tries to pick me up again, but she fails. Jason stops as well and stares at me and then looks at Renée.

"What's the matter with him?" he asks coldly.

The vibrations are more intense. The crackling sound of wood snapping can be heard.

Booooom!

The staircase explodes into a billion splinters. Alina is grabbed by a huge monster and dragged into the cave system below.

"*Alina!*" scream Jason and Renée.

Renée grabs Jason as he tries to rush towards Alina. Jason is distraught.

"She ordered us to get them out," commands Renée.

Jason grabs Andrew while Renée picks me up again.

She musters all her energy and lets out a brief sigh. She grinds her teeth as she lifts me to my feet. I am able to get back on my feet with a lot – I mean a *lot* of help from Renée. The pain has weakened. I think it has something to do with the guardian. We race to an exit as fast as possible. I can still hear Alina; I try to search for her below. The cave system is too deep. I can see a very faint light below, but it vanishes.

"You hear me, don't you? I know you can. I always knew you could. I hope you can see me down here. I just want to tell you. I am sorry. I wish I was a better friend. One who should have told you that you should never have joined us. This is my last message to you, my dear friend, Ajay. I watched a sweet, innocent person turn so cold over these years. I know the pain you are going through, but I should have never fuelled your hatred for these monsters to this point. I know it's too late. I know the bloodlust is too strong, but you need to let go of the hate. I am now here, staring at this beast. My fate and hate have led me to this place. I stare at the enemy that stole my life, the life of two beautiful children, my love, my parents and my friends; each one fell victim to these blood and soul-sucking monsters. I lost everything and, at this moment, staring at this monster with its teeth in my neck, I can only think that, if only I chose a different path… this would not by my final moment. I'm going to take one last pull on my joint, blow the smoke at this bitch and…" says Alina.

Renée puts Ajay in the back of a truck filled with books and the vampire guard from earlier.

Alina continues, "You can trust Renée."

The ground rumbles as if another earthquake has struck, followed by the sound of an explosion that comes from the cave system. I cannot hear her anymore, but I can hear the guardian's screams as it burns in the cave system.

I remember her words. *You can trust Renée.*

I can only watch as Renée and a group of men rush towards the building. I turn to the vampire guard. The hunger has returned with a vengeance.

Her words echo. *Let go of the hate.*

I know what you lost, Alina, but they took more from me than just the death of a loved one. They turned me into the thing that killed my loved one, Ria – that is more horrifying and painful than anything you can ever imagine. I see the book from earlier, *Evolution of Species* by Dr X Martin. I turn to the vampire guard again and grab him by the neck.

"Female vampire. Blonde… *where is she?*" I demand.

"No such thing," he arrogantly says.

"Please say that again," I say as I show him my fangs.

"What are you?" he asks as his arrogance turns to fear.

"Fear… *Blonde female,*" I reply as I press on his neck.

He tries to scream, but cannot due to the pressure of my grip on his neck.

* * *

Renée returns to the truck.

"Ajay, how are you feeling?" she asks as she opens the back of the truck, only to find the vampire guard gasping for air in the corner of the truck.

Ajay is gone. Renée looks around the area as Jason brings Andrew and puts him in the truck.

"Where is he?" he asks.

CHAPTER SIX

Sometimes Not Even Death Can Contain Us

That was forty-seven years ago. So much has changed. I am now seated in the same room as Renée, a now de-werewolved Alex and Ria… Ria… How…? How is this possible? I am still trying to fight this urge to turn back into the beast. A fight I might lose or I might overcome. I can smell the blood in Alex. I can see him trying not to go all wolfed out. A tear, one single lonely tear rolls down my face and falls to the floor. I am trying so hard. I… I just… *I just want to rip out his soul…* but I cannot. You have to hold in the urge. I keep staring at him, but my gaze shifts to Ria. She is standing and taking to Renée. Is she real? I am confused. How is she real? I killed her… right? I am chained to the wall, but that has never been an issue for me before. I examine the shackles and then look at Ria. She is looking back at me.

She looks exactly like she did on that night on the porch, but also so different. It is her aura. She is still looking at me.

* * *

I look at him, my Ajay. It does not feel like him anymore. He is so different. I can feel the pain inside him. I feel his rage, but, every once in a while when he looks back at me, I feel my Ajay, the sweet, caring, beautiful soul. I knew when I came back that this road would not be easy. I have spent so much time fighting through the barriers and dimensions to reach him. I would have fought against the entire universe just to see him, my Ajay.

I turn back to Renée, who does not seem fazed by all of the supernatural beings in her presence.

"How are you here?" asks an extremely curious Renée.

"It was not an easy journey," I reply. "I just hope my presence here can change a path that was taken. He is so lost from the young man I once knew. The years have been unkind to all of us, but the rage I feel from him scares me. I hope I am not too late to save him."

How do I relate my true journey through all that I have been through to get to this point?

This story goes back to that night in my bedroom. You were there, remember, Ajay. Of course you do, but do you know the pain and confusion I was in when I was bitten on my neck? I tried to yell, but I could not; all I could feel was your pain and your hunger. I should have yelled, but I knew I was too late. I could see the horror in your eyes when you let go. My emotions were at an all-time high. I was enraged. How could you? How could the person I love so much ever do this to me? Those were the thoughts that ran through my head as I disintegrated in front of you. Of all the emotions that I had during my final moments, the one that stood out the most was how much I hated you... I hated you. The person I trust and love so much, you, my Ajay, you broke all of that. How could you? It felt like the moment I took my final breath was the moment I woke up from this nightmare.

I was back on the porch. I was back in that moment in time with you staring at me, still with so much love in your eyes. We were getting closer to each other, but this time was different. This time, the door did not open. You grabbed my hand and placed your other hand on my face. I could feel your firm, but soft touch on my face. We got closer. I could feel your breath on my face as we kissed for the very first time. This time, this night happened exactly how it was meant to happen. I was there in your arms and I held on to you as tight as I could. This felt like heaven. My lips on yours; this was our moment. I flashed through every moment we should have had together. Our second date – it would have been in a fancy restaurant by the pier. We laughed and you just gazed at me. We were at the beach; you were on your knee with a ring in your hand. I looked at you and the ring. You said, "Marry me." I nodded. It was such a beautiful moment. You jumped up to your feet in excitement, grabbed me by the waist and kissed me. We were then in a temple – you know, like in those Bollywood movies. It was covered in strings of marigold flowers. A majestic blaze of orange and yellow. I looked at my hands, which were covered in mehndi. My parents were at my side. I could hear the pundit reciting something. I was not paying attention him; at that moment, I could see just you. You were behind me as we walked around the fire. You were in a suit and a turban. You looked funny. I nudged you with my elbow and motioned with my eyes to the turban. You looked at me and smirked at me before rolling your eyes at me. We laughed at each other. I closed my eyes and there you were again, but now we were in what looked like a hospital room. I was on the bed.

What's going on? What's happening? I see you, but your back is to me. There is a nurse before you; it looks like you are holding something. What is it? Am I dying? Why am I here? You turn to me. Is that…? No, it can't be. You are holding a baby. You place her in my arms. I gaze upon her as if I know her, as if she was this massive part of my past, present and future. You just look at me. I am confused, but ecstatic. She is perfect. She has a tag on her foot. The tag states 'Ahana'. That is you, little one. Ahana. She grabs my finger and I close my eyes and, as I open my eyes, I am now at the bottom of a staircase and there you are, Ajay. You stand right here by my side. You are much older. I just stare at you watching your face. You stare back at me with a smile.

"Mum," says a voice from the top of the stairs.

I look up the stairs. I see a pretty young lady; she must by around seventeen or eighteen years old. She is wearing a stunning green dress. She has long hazel hair. She looks like me when I was her age.

"What do you think?" she asks to me with a gigantic smile. She seems so excited and bubbly.

"Stunning, Ahana," I say, with tears rolling down my cheeks. These are tears of joy. I am happy.

She walks down the stairs.

"Ria!" I hear a voice call to me.

I turn to the door and now I am on the bridge.

I see Ajay on the bridge. He sees me, but he is just staring at me and I stare at him. I move towards him, trying to call out to him, but I cannot. I hold out my hand to him while still trying to get closer to him. I try once more to call out to him, but something holds onto me.

"Aaaaaaaaaarrrrrr!" I let out a deathly scream and close my eyes.

I am back on the porch. I am back on the porch?

What the hell is going on? How did I get back here?

Ajay is standing before me. Why am I back on this porch again? I just saw him a few moments ago on the bridge. This Ajay before me is different. Why is there blood on his shirt? I look down and I have blood on my shirt too. I grab my neck and then look at my hand and it is covered in blood. No, no, no... Not again. I look at Ajay and there is blood on his face. He has a weird look in his eyes. He looks at me like his favourite pizza. I hear a knock at the door and, before he can grab me again, I reach for the door knob and open the door and now I am back at the bottom of the stairs.

"Mum," says a voice from the top of the stairs.

I know that voice. Ajay is next to me and I grab his arm. I look at him, but we are no more in the house at the bottom of the stairs. Where are we? I can see a crematorium and I stand here on this hilltop next to Ajay. He looks a tad confused and scared. He stares at me and then I am pulled back to the porch once again. Is this real?

You are here again with me on this porch. I blink and I am back in the hospital bed with baby Ahana in my arms. She looks so peaceful. My attention turns back to the door, but, this time, I can hear a song. This is something that I have never heard before. What is it? It is hauntingly beautiful. I blink and I am back at the bottom of the stairs.

"Mom!" she calls.

The song... it is still here. It is coming from the door.

The song plays – Memories – Within Temptation.

"Mom!" she calls once more.

The door is tempting me. I look at Ahana; she is beautiful on those stairs, but that song is drowning out this moment as I hear it intently. I hear more of the song that is drawing me in as I go to open the door.

"Mom!" Ahana yells from the stairs.

I am still drawn to the door and the song that is playing on the other side. I am pulled towards the door and I have to know… I just have to know.

"Mom!" she yells once more.

I am here now at the door and I turn the knob and open the door.

I am here. Where is this? I am not outside the house. I do not see a yard or the neighbourhood. This place is so cold, but I can still hear the song playing.

"Mom!" she calls to me.

I turn to her and she stands there glaring at me with those innocent eyes. The song continues to play. I smile at her, but walk through the door as the song words are sung. It looks like a lab and there he is, my Ajay. He is sitting there so lost, just listening to the song playing. That is where the song is coming from. I can feel the coldness inside him. He sees me and smiles.

"Beautiful song," he says as I smile back at him.

I hear a loud wolf-like howl echo in the next room. Ajay jumps to his feet. He stares at me fearfully. As I am being pulled back to the porch, I catch a glimpse of the date on a calendar on the wall: 2014.

I understand now. This porch, this place, this Ajay is not real. The one out there seems much darker, but I feel a small part of him. Fake Ajay moves closer to me, but I push him back and lunge forward to the doorknob. I am transported to a hallway. I see him, my Ajay, but there is less of him in this version. I can still feel a part of the old Ajay. His soul feels tortured and beastly. I try to say something.

"Let the pain go." My words echo through the room.

He gazes back at me and I hear his whisper. "I wish I could." He falls to his knee and repeats, "I wish I could."

I am being pulled back once more, but I am not in the mood for this. I fight back at the hand that tries to pull me. I want to get back to him. I am back in the hallway. Ajay is being attacked by three men. I just watch as a once sweet, innocent soul has now turned into a vicious, sadistic monster.

He looks back at me and says, "This is going to be messy."

He rips through the skull of one of his attackers. I am once again pulled back to the staircase.

"Mom!" she calls out to me.

I look at her and then at the door, which has now become a beacon of hope – hope that I will return to my Ajay. I rush to the door and now I am at an entrance to a mine. I can feel death all around me, but I can also feel life. However, the stench of death lingers in the air. There is an explosion with a bellowing scream echoing through the mine and into the town. I rush into the cave.

"Ajay!" I yell.

I don't see him. There is debris everywhere. I can feel you, but where are you? I search frantically. I can still feel you. There is something… there in the rubble… There is a hand. I rush to him and grab his hand. What is going on? I am holding his hand, but how is this possible? I can hold him. I was only ever able to use this life force to touch him. I try to pull him from the rubble. There he is. He is still alive. Winded, but okay.

He opens his eyes and says, "Ria."

I am pulled back to the staircase once more. There she is once again on the staircase, Ahana in that dress, but, this time, there is no door behind me.

"Mom," she says.

I look at her and at the top of the staircase.

"I want nothing more in my life than for you to have been my daughter. This life… I wanted this more than anything. Ajay, you and me standing here in this moment; that is all I ever wanted. Growing old with my Ajay and spending eternity right here. That is all I wanted," I say to Ahana as I slowly walk up the stairs with tears streaming down my face.

"Why can you not have all of that and more?" she asks.

"You are all I want. He is everything to me, but this is all a lie. My Ajay is out there. He calls to my soul. I cannot pretend that this is true when the real Ajay is not the one at the bottom of the stairs," I reply as I get to her on the stairs.

"You cannot leave," she commands.

"I love him more than this illusion and, no matter what you do to try to keep me here, I will defy you every step of the way. He needs me and now I know I can do so much more than just stand there. Now either get out of my way or I just go through you," I reply defiantly.

"You would forsake Heaven for him," says Ahana.

"Without him, there is no Heaven," I say as I walk through the light at the top of the staircase.

I am now outside. It is windy and I see monsters before me. I see Ajay. He turns to me.

"Hey," I say as I gaze into his eyes.

I gave up Paradise, but what is the worth of Paradise without him? He is right beside me now. The rest is up to us.

Something About a Werewolf

How is she here? She stands next to Renée. She is not my imagination; she is real. I look at Alex. Ria is walking towards me. She places her hand on my face. I can feel her. She is real. I can feel tears roll down my face.

"Hey," she says.

I am emotional and turn my head away from her in shame. I know what I have become. She will be so disappointed in me.

All I can utter is, "Monster."

She walks away from me, but glances at me. I can see the pain in her eyes. She must think of me as such a monster. I have to become human again even just for a moment so

I can die knowing that she does not see the monster she sees now.

I look at Alex once more.

"Bastard. I wish to rip you apart. Why do you stare at me so?" asks Alex.

I examine him. "You have not changed in appearance."

"What does that mean? You do not know me!" he yells.

I am confused. Why does he not remember me?

"You don't remember?" I ask curiously as he rattles his chains.

"Remember? All I see is something that has to die," he says with malice.

"Alexandré Evans, born 13 July 1988. Your father was British, John Evans. He was a tailor in France, where he met your mother, Aveline Moreau, a chef at a restaurant in Lyon," I say.

"This means nothing to me, Evil," he utters.

"You truly don't remember." I look at him, puzzled.

He shakes his head.

"Alex… Alex, I am so sorry. If we knew…" I say.

"You act as if you know me. You even know my name. How?" he asks curiously.

"I meant you when you were 24 years old. You worked for Doctor Xanthias Martin," I say as I see his eyes light up.

"Dr Martin; he wore a patch on his left eye," he says as he is trying to remember the past.

"You do remember!" I exclaim.

He stares at me as if he is looking directly into my soul.

"Ajay!"

He remembers as the realisation of who he is rushes through his mind like a massive tsunami raging through the land, destroying the fortresses built within his mind. All those constructs, built over the last twenty years, begin to be swept away as this torrent of memories and emotions that came before he forgot who he was comes flooding back. He is unable to control his emotions. He cannot contain the conflict that rages within. I look at Renée and Ria and back at Alex. That conflict within him is going to fuel the rage that powers the wolf.

He twitches.

"*Ria!*" I yell as I look at her and then Alex, who is in the midst of his transformation.

He yells. He bones crack as his fingers extend and become more pointed. His mouth stretches out. He continues to yell through the pain.

Ria looks at Alex and then she creates a vortex around him, draining the air out of the vortex. Alex is fading fast. The barely transformed werewolf falls to his knees with the chains holding him, preventing him from hitting the floor.

* * *

I wandered the Earth for more than twenty years from the last time I saw Renée. Every day, more of me died bit by bit as the monster within raged through all those who stood before me, simply just to quench this lust and hunger for blood. I have searched for the thing that made me this way, but I am still no closer to finding that female vampire. During the course of my journey, I discovered that the idea of a female vampire being real was like chasing an impossible dream. I dragged myself through two decades, bleeding dry all sorts of vampires and monsters and some not even the type you would believe were monsters – those who preyed on helpless innocence. I was innocent once too; the only difference is that my monster is a true definition of the word monster. Unlike those things you see in the movies. This world is too sick and I wish I could say I regretted any moment. I have felt my soul slowly die, but the desire to wrap my fangs around the neck of that vampire remains stronger now than ever. My journey has now become twofold: revenge and death. My revenge has led me to this place…

PARIS, FRANCE, 2012

The year 2012 – what a weird year. I spend most of my time in Poland. Weirdly, there are tons of vampires, so my travel becomes a stay of almost two months. I have an amazing time eating my way through the Polish cities. I give a new meaning to the words 'paint the town red'. The next stop on my blood tour is Paris. It takes me a long time to track down a specific doctor.

At this moment in time, most people are convinced the world will end. Why would they not believe that when the Mayan calendar made a prediction of great disasters that would rip apart the world? Funny; not laugh out loud funny – more like just how crazy they must be to believe in something so stupid. Anyway, back to where I am. Ah, yes. Paris in June. Summer has begun. The city is so vibrant and alive, but I can see so much more. I can feel them beneath the streets like the vermin scurrying under the city. How lucky are they? My mission is not about those soul suckers. My focus is on Doctor Xanthias Martin. I hunted for as much information on the doctor as I could find in the last two decades. I read as much of his research as I could get my hands on. He made me believe in something as crazy as this doctor's work could cure me of this curse. I have my doubts – maybe there is no way to find this man's research. Someone has to know more about the doctor or maybe a descendant who knew how to conduct his experiments. If I cannot be cured, maybe his work can kill me or the vampire for whom I have searched for decades. I wish I was closer, but I am not any closer than I was to her that night when she changed my life forever.

I finally have one lead. I heard of this young man who can help me. He is a bright student who posts his work on the dark web. He bases a lot of his findings and work on Dr Martin's research. The experiments were very extreme and talked about gene manipulation. As if it is simple as mixing ingredients in a bowl and producing a new species with a few tweaks to the recipe. It sounds radical, but what intrigued me the most was that they mentioned they used vampiric blood to stabilise the concoction to create the new evolutionary jump the genes needed. It sounds like science fiction, but, when I analyse the data with Dr Martins work, it all lines up perfectly. The hope is that this twenty-four-year-old student is going to be my saving grace and it will all happen here in Paris. I began contacting Alex more than two years ago; he initially brushed me off as some weirdo conspiracy nut. I still question how he knew so much. Was he a student of Dr Martin? Then again, how is that possible? Dr Martin would be more than 300 years old by now. Even vampires cannot live that long. I hope not; that would mean… No, no, not possible. I will not accept that. They must be able to die. I must be able to die.

Possible, says the voice.

"Quiet!" I reply. "You don't get to dictate what happens from this point on."

You failed to listen. Now look at yourself, a vagrant roaming the Earth like a mindless zombie, thirsty for blood and trying desperately to be something you cannot return to. Our humanity is dead, retorts the voice.

Not listening anymore. We have a meeting with Alex at around 3pm at the Eiffel Tower.

Faces continue to pass by unaware of the world that lives right before them. A world so deadly and dangerous that it shatters our existence on this planet. I fail once again to pay attention to the beauty that surrounds this place; all I feels is this dreaded hunger brewing inside me. People continue to pass by and, with each face that passes, the hunger grows stronger. I am fighting as much as I can, but this city is full of life, full of blood. It smells so sweet. Her… I can smell her sweet-scented blood. No… No… No… Her… No… That guy there… They all smell… They smell so… *Get it together, Ajay!*

I remain here on this park bench struggling to hold on as more people walk by. I am still waiting for Alex. I wish I could beat this urge, but, of all the urges, the one for vampire blood is being tested the most. They are under the streets; I can feel them. I just want to sink my fangs into their corpses. I just… I Just… I…

"Ajay," says a voice in front of me.

How did I not notice him? The bloodlust has blinded my sight. How did I not see him?

"Alex?" I reply as I look at this 6-foot-2 man. He is blonde, with a pale white complexion and a very French accent. He sits next to me.

"*Enfin, on se recontre.*[4] Welcome to Paris. *Tu dois avoir beaucoup de questions sur mon travail,*"[5] says Alex.

There is something about him; it is subtle, something in his blood. I can smell it. The only strange thing is that he does not glow like Andrew does, but I get a similar sense from him. It is faint and a bit unsettling.

"*J'ai beaucoup à te montrer et quelqu'un que je veux que tu rencontres,*"[5] says Alex as he stands up and leads us away from the Eiffel Tower.

I keep thinking about what he is going to show me and about this person he wants me to meet.

We walk for a while. I can still feel them below the streets. We are now in an alley. This alley is alive with people and businesses. Alex is a lively person. He is joyous and funny; his English does need some work, though. I cannot help

---

4 "Finally, we meet."
5 "You must have many questions about my work."
6 "I have a lot to show you and someone I want you to meet."

but be jealous just a tad. I mean, look at all these people and this young man. He has his whole life in the palms of his hands and the world, for him, responds with showers of love and admiration of this soul.

A shopkeeper notices Alex.

"Alex, *mon gars, comment ça va?*"[7] asks the shopkeeper.

"Monsieur Laurent, ça va bien Comment va Madame Laurent?"[8] replies Alex.

"*Elle va bien Elle est partie à Marseille pour voir Georgina Ça fait un moment qu'on ne t'a pas vu,*"[9] says Mr Laurent.

"*Travail, travail et encore du travail Comment vont Georgina et Olivia?*"[10] asks Alex.

"*Ils vont bien Georgina est la directrice financière de l'entreprise et Olivia vient de commencer l'école,*"[11] says Mr Laurent.

"Wow, ça fait trop longtemps Je passerai ce soir,"[12] says Alex as we walk to a stairway leading to a lower level of the alleyway.

---

7 "My guy, how are you?"

8 "How is Madame Laurent doing?"

9 "She's fine. She went to Marseilles to see Georgina. It's been a while since we last saw you."

10 "Work, work, and more work. How are Georgina and Olivia?"

11 "They are doing well. Georgina is the financial director of the company and Olivia has just started school."

12 "It's been too long. I'll stop by this evening."

"That is Mr Laurent. He runs the store with his wife. She has gone to stay with her daughter, Georgina, and their granddaughter, Olivia. Nice people," says Alex.

We head towards a lower gate. I am looking at it from a different view; it is a cave system.

"Are we in the catacombs?" I ask as I continue to scan the area.

I know the bloodsuckers are here somewhere; wait a second, maybe he… No, Ajay. He smells different. Just be on your guard, Ajay.

"Yes. Do not worry; they do not come here," he replies as he opens a secret door in one of the walls covered in skulls – humanoid skulls.

I should pay more attention to my surroundings, but I don't really care about that right now. I look at Alex.

"What do you mean?" I ask curiously, as if I do not know what he's talking about.

"Vampires, Ajay. The bloody vampires that have been lurking in the catacombs. That is what you have been searching for," says a voice from inside the hallway.

He has an accent with which I am unfamiliar. He sounds Middle Eastern with a hint of Ancient Greek. I stare down the hallway at this man – an elderly gentleman, roughly 80 years old, with a patch on his left eye. He also has a limp on his right side and, therefore, he has an amazing crafted cane. The cane has a wolf made of silver on it. He does not glow like everyone else. He has no glow. I cannot see him, but he has a distinct scent. I can smell it in his blood; there… right there; just a hint of it. A faint hint of vampire in there. He is not a vampire, but may have gone through the same or similar process to alter his DNA.

"Dr Martin," I say as I look at Alex and then at Dr Martin. "I have been searching for you for years."

"I know, Ajay; we just needed to be sure first," he replies.

We walk into the lab and my thoughts remain on this man and Alex. My focus needs to be sharp – what if this is a trap? Exit – I need to find all exits. No other way out but the way we came in. It may be harder than it looks to escape. I cannot access the exit if these two are potentially stronger than the average vampire is, but, if I use Andrew as a gauge, this might end up being an intense battle. I can easily take the younger one, but it is Mr Wolf Cane over there – there is something sinister about him.

"You seem suspicious of me. Why, may I ask, is that, Ajay?" asks Dr Martin as he scans me.

"As I have said, I have searched for you for a long time, but, over the years, I began to believe that finding you was not a possibility," I reply, still scanning the room and the two men. I thought this would be impossible, but that would also mean that my fate is…

"Alex, we need some supper. Will you arrange that?" asks Dr Martin.

Alex begins to walk to the door and heads back out into the catacombs. The door behind him closes.

Dr Martin peers at me. "You were saying…?"

"Does the boy know who you really are?" I ask blatantly.

"He knows enough. May I enquire what you are insinuating?" asks the Dr Martin as he walks towards his desk.

"Dr Xanthias Martin, or should I just call you Xanthias? An Ancient Greek scientist and philosopher from 365 BC. You look well for a person over two millennia old. I am still scanning you to understand what type of being can survive that long. One is a vampire; you do have a hint of it in your blood, but not enough… so hybrid, maybe. The only question I have now is which side is this hybrid on?" I ask the doctor.

He looks at me, emotionless. He is still scanning me as well. He is most probably thinking the same things about me.

"I have been pondering the same about you. You are not that old, but that smell from you tells me that there is more than what I initially thought was in you. There was something similar to you almost a millennium ago. You and this creature should never have existed. The reason for that being was the failure of the guardian to dispose of you. The guardians – those hideous, vile creatures. Imagine these things were once guardian angels, beings that are attached to every being. They are there as silent watchers that continue to guide people through life. A vampire is born on a rare occurrence and their births happen once every few cycles. With vampires, it is very different; vampires are born due to a mutation in their genetic coding that creates a deficiency that requires blood. This transformation also causes a violent change in the guardian angel as they are hurtled out of the gates of the Afterworld. They are banished to Earth to protect their wards. The idea in books and movies that the vampire creates another by bite is false. Due to the mutation of the genes, when vampires bites someone, they create a blood-lusting vampire killer. A monster that is far more deadly and unpredictable. The guardian protects its ward by devouring the victim's soul and body, thereby killing the monster they may become. However, in 1082, a vampire was feeding on a person when a group of villagers killed the vampire and, in doing so, they saved the victim, or so they thought. A few days later, when the young woman woke up, she was bloodthirsty and killed several people in her village. When a vampire bites you, what remains is a violent being driven by hunger for blood," says Xanthias.

"What happened to the woman?" I ask as I walk towards Xanthias.

"Unfortunately for her, the guardian found her and ripped her to shreds," replies Xanthias.

This shakes me to my core. My hands are still shaking. This makes me think of Alina and her words: *When you hear a second, you run.* These combined words echo through my soul. As much as I want to die, I still have one purpose. Kill the vampire that made me this way.

"I have come to you for one reason. How do we kill them all? Guardians and vampires?" I ask him.

"I have a way," says Xanthias as Alex walks through the door. "There is a beast… Alex, my boy, show Ajay what we have been working on." Xanthias walks to a door at the back of the lab.

Alex looks at me and then guides me through the door. A new world of possibilities awaits in the next room. It is a world that will alter the course of all our lives over the next two years. I still remember the vile smell of death and despair. The stench… I cannot get over the smell of rot and decay of the failed attempts to create this beast able to kill both vampire and guardian. The process is painstaking; the screams still haunt me.

* * *

My humanity is still intact, but just barely; the hunger fights back at me as much as I fight with it, desperately trying to hold it back. We are constantly around those vile vampires.

The hope within the team fades in the last two years. We began this journey with stars in our eyes and a hatred of vampires. Now, we have limited test subjects – scratch that; we have no more test subjects.

I look at Alex carrying out another disfigured, headless mutation. He looks lost as he walks through the door with the lifeless body draped over his shoulder.

* * *

This evening, Alex and I sit at the restaurant in the alleyway. Alex waves at Mr Laurent, who is across the road.

"End of the road; that is what this feels like. Maybe it is the people we have been using. It must take someone special to be mutated in such a fashion that they survive the tormenting process as their bodies transform into a new beast. My mind always goes back to a man I once met. He was so weakened by the process, but he was so much of a fighter that, no matter what was done to him, he fought with all his soul to overcome and endure the torture he went through. It is an ineffable mystery as to how he survived," I say to Alex as we sit there in hopelessness.

He looks at me with a glimmer of awe. "You are an ineffable force of nature yourself. In all probability, you, Ajay… you should never have been here either."

I ponder how true his remarks are. How am I able to survive, not only the bite, but also every attempt I made to end my life. Why is he staring at me? I know that look; it means he is about to do something that he should not.

"You have that odd look again, Alex," I say as he looks down the alleyway.

"We have nothing to lose at this point. I believe I have an idea that should work," says Alex as he stands up with a renewed hope. "*Merde.* Let's go."

* * *

We sit in the lab, the same lab with books and research papers lying all around us. There are vials of blood and beakers of chemicals all through the lab. I am there with Xanthias and Alex. I see Alex's mouth moving, but I am not focussed on what he is saying. I continue to think about one thing: failing. If we fail tonight, two years have been wasted on creating something that does not exist. I need to focus. I look back at Alex.

"…Mixing blood does not just form creatures. You cannot mix different blood types; the reaction would be fatal to the host subject, but, if we mixed vampire DNA with each blood we mix, this would break down the DNA structure and allow it to rebuild into a new DNA structure. We would have to use the DNA mix and use a part mix of vampire DNA again before injecting it into the host," says Alex.

"This might just be possible," says Xanthias.

"What about using my blood?" I ask.

"I have analysed it before; there are missing pieces in your DNA. How you are alive with DNA built in this fashion is beyond my understanding. The effect of adding your DNA to the mix would create a creature with unknown effects," says Xanthias.

"What if we us me, Dr Martin?" asks Alex as he walks towards the vials of blood on the table. "As we established, we just need to introduce vampire blood into my blood and then introduce the blood of a creature that could hunt vampires and then, as you introduce more vampire blood, we use high-voltage power."

"What creature could hunt vampires?" I ask as Xanthias walks to Alex.

There is something about the relationship between the teacher and student that reassures me that I may have made the right choice.

"I have that one covered, but, Alex, I have to ask you once more. Are you sure?" asks Xanthias, who seems slightly concerned about this path.

I have seen Alex broken and tired, but today is different. Today, he seems optimistic and hopeful. He is not afraid of the possibility of death. He looks at me and then at Xanthias and simply just nods in affirmation. It seems all systems are a go.

"This is history in the making. This beast we are about to create will be able to hunt its target like a lion stalking its prey," says Xanthias, overly excited by the thought of his beast being a reality.

"Perfect hunter; it would not rest until it kills its target?" I ask Xanthias in the hope that he will… I don't know what I am hoping he will say.

"Once it locates its target, it will be relentless," he says to me as he grabs the research papers and turns to Alex. "Alex, it is time. Ajay, can you bring in the other samples?" He walks to the inner lab.

I make my way to the desk and grab the vials of blood sitting on it. I lose myself staring at the vials. The thoughts of different consequences to my actions run wildly. This is a beast that could kill me, but is it able to without including my blood in the mix? I have to… The probability of me being immortal is a very strong fear that is now becoming more of a nightmarish reality. 'What if' scenarios flood my mind, running through every outcome. The thoughts rage. What if, after everything, I finally kill that vampire lady and nothing changes? What if I never find that lady vampire and I continue to roam this world until the end of time and then I still remain alive in a void of emptiness, trapped by this curse for eternity? Without Ria, this world has got so much darker. I have become so much darker. This darkness shrouds my soul in hopeless emptiness. I have to…

"Ajay!" calls Alex from the inner lab, his voice urgent.

I have to make a quick decision.

* * *

It is now late December 2014. Xanthias and Alex have prepared the blood samples that will be injected into Alex before he is zapped with more than a trillion volts – an over-exaggeration, but, to him, it will definitely fucking feel like it. I sit in the outer lab, all alone. The radio is playing a song. Alex loves his playlists. He does have some great taste in music. *Memories – Within Temptation* is playing. I love this song; it is so beautiful. As the song begins, all I can focus on is Ria and that night on the porch. How could all of this happen? I can hear Alex and Xanthias as they walk through the procedure. What have I done? I lose myself again staring at the floor. There is a light by the door. I hear the song lyrics. My gaze slowly rises to the light. I see her: Ria. I smile at her. She looks normal, more like the Ria I once knew.

"Beautiful song," I say to her.

I hear Xanthias pull the switch in the inner lab.

Hooooowwwwllll!

I hear a loud wolf-like howl echo through the cave. I jump up to my feet look at Ria. I am trembling. What the fuck did I do? I look at her again and she vanishes. The howl grows louder.

Xanthias screams, "*What have we done? Alex, my boy. Alex… Alex… Please, no!*"

Those are the last words of an immortal being screaming before his final breath.

Farewell, Xanthias.

I can feel the vibration on the floor. I can't see him, but I can feel him. I am next; no time to think this one through.

"*Run, Ajay, run!*" I yell at myself as I hear the beast's footsteps.

I race out of the door and into the cave system. How fast can I run? That monster is a heat-seeking missile and right now I am the heat that it is seeking. Think, dummy, think.

Vampire! We are surrounded by vampires. I need to get to a place that has a lot of them, tons of them; that would cause it to focus on them and not me.

"Run," I whisper as I race deeper into the cave system.

I can see them. Yes, this will do perfectly. I can now smell them; they smell so… *No!* I need to focus and I need to control this hunger or that beast is going to kill me. They are in what seems like a large cavern in the cave system. I run past it and hide as deep as I can in a dusty part of a broken wall. It runs into the room. I hear their cries as the beast devours his way through the room. The sounds of their screams vibrates across the cave system. This would have shaken me to my soul when I was human; so much has changed in these last twenty years. I keep thinking how much of my humanity is left as I hear the screams further off in the distance. I cannot remember how long I am in that crevice; I focus only on the cries. I move one step at a time, cautiously. That's a lie. I am still trembling in fear. After all these years, nothing has scared me more than that beast does. I drag myself back to the lab only to find the carnage we brought upon the world. What have I done? My foot knocks into what looks like a limb. I scan the room, searching for the rest of Dr Martin. Blood splatters and stains plaster the walls as if someone did a bad job painting the place. There lies Xanthias' head, a few feet away from the destroyed lab tables. We did it. We created the perfect hunter, but at what cost? Now, Alex is out there somewhere.

"I have to find him," I say to myself.

And if you do, you will die, says the voice in my head.

"I cannot let him loose out there in the world. Look at this place. Look at the devastation he can cause," I say.

Death it is, then, says the voice.

I chose to die the moment I chose to add my blood to that concoction.

* * *

I search the catacombs for almost three years. Through my journey, the only thing I find is death. That is exactly what I brought to the world ever since that night. Every person I get close to eventually ends up dead, or worse, they become death itself. This curse has taken everything from me. I know our paths will eventually cross once more, but, until then, I will continue to kill every vampire. No more shortcuts. They all die.

CHAPTER EIGHT

All Roads Lead Here

Renée and Ria are talking. My gaze is focussed on Alex as he is beginning to remember the last twenty-odd years of his life. I can see the horror in his eyes; he must have got to the part where he killed Xanthias. I turned him into a…

* * *

Ria

"Monster," I say to Renée as I glance at Ajay, who is held to the floor by chains in the wall.

"He called me a monster. He could barely look at me. I catch him on occasion staring at me and then turning away as if he hates what I have become," I say as I look at Ajay once more.

* * *

Ajay

I see Ria. I cannot believe she is here. She keeps looking back at me. How can I look at her? She must think…

* * *

Ria

"Monster, Renée. That is what he said," I say, feeling the stream of tears roll down my cheeks. I place my hand on my cheeks, wiping away my shame.

* * *

"You misunderstand. The monster he speaks of is not you. I know what he has gone through. We would often talk when he was in the basement. The years may have passed, but I still see some of what he used to be in there. The pain is still there. He never forgave himself for what he did to you. How could he? He killed the person he loved the most in this world. He is not ashamed of what you have become; he is ashamed that you have seen what he has become as he navigated this life trying desperately to reverse this curse. He feels that you hate what he has become. He is the monster he speaks of," says Renée as she holds Ria's hand and turns to Ajay.

"But I love him. I fought through multiple dimensions to come back for him," says Ria.

"And he loves you so much that he darkened his soul to find the thing that can return him to his humanity before he dies," replies Renée.

Ria walks to Ajay. She holds his head to hers. She stares into his eyes and he is forced to look her in her eyes too.

"I love you, Ajay," she says.

His eyes becomes misty and tears stream down his face. He looks away and says, "Still a monster."

"I still *love you!*" she says to Ajay.

"How do we break this curse?" asks Renée as Ajay and Alex are released from their chains.

"Can you handle the beast for a while?" I ask Alex.

He nods at me.

"The next step in our journey lies in a place with which we are both familiar," I say to the group as I turn to Renée.

"What do you mean?" asks Renée.

"Bell Tower Mansion. I felt a presence last night after we encountered the guardians. I think it is her," I say as I walk over to the war room table.

"Why there?" asks Renée as she moves over to the table.

Ria stands a bit further back and Alex remains in the doorway.

"After my last transition, I am now able to sense much more than before. The cave system below is a hive. There are multiple layers to the system as it goes below. We are going to need an army to get to the level below. There are a few thousand vampires on the floors above, and then there are the guardians on the second level, a third level and finally a single chamber at the bottom. That's where I felt that presence. She is there," I say as I look around the room scanning the faces of the people who I am asking to risk everything for me to end this saga that has spanned more than half a century.

I know this must not seem like much, but every minute I have been alive has had a ripple effect on the lives with which I have come into contact. I am hoping for a miracle at this point.

Renée sighs. "I wish we had that many. This place is not as it used to be. We have maybe a hundred or so men and Andrew."

"Disappointing, to say the least, but, with three super-powered beings, it will be difficult," I say.

"*Mérde.* I have something that may work," says Alex.

"What?" asks Ria.

"Let us call it a surprise for now," replies Alex.

Renée turns to me. She has a concerned look on her face. "That is it? Are you sure this is what you want to do?"

I glance at Alex and Ria. Is this what I want? No… but my choice is limited; I cannot remain as this monster any longer.

"We have to move now," I command.

This is the moment I get back my humanity. I searched for almost half a century. She is there… She has to be or all of this time, all of these will be in vain. I did not spend all this time and effort to be let down now. I have to be human again. I have to… even just for a second. No more bloodlust; no more will I be this monster.

* * *

It is now dusk. We are outside the abandoned mansion once again. Imagine, after all these years, I have come back here. This journey was to get back my humanity so I could be with her, and here she is. That should be enough. It would be enough for anyone else, but why is it not enough for me? I know this makes no sense, but all of this was to be with Ria. No matter how many times I stare at her, it just seems like something is missing inside me; that part, the part she loved, is gone. I have destroyed that bit and the only salvation I have now is that this curse can be broken by that lady vampire's death. I turn to Alex, who is standing at the edge away from all of us. I can see his struggles; I know his struggles. The lust for blood and death suffocates us.

"Move in," I command the troops that are behind us.

"Should I call them?" asks Alex as he moves towards the mansion.

"Not yet," I say as I scan the ground and I see Alex doing the same. "We have a lot of levels to get to. For now, just hold them until I say so."

I step through the mansion doors, renewed with hope, something I thought I lost along with the last part of my soul. I scan the building.

Well, at least the damage to the building seems to be repaired, unlike your soul, says the voice in my head. Funny, it still has a sense of humour.

So far, so good; no vampires in sight as we make our way down to the cave system below. The staircase is repaired. I remember that night as if it was yesterday; that is why, when I look at Ria, I remember the night on the porch. I remember her smile… her laugh… that sparkle in her eyes. I remember looking at her lips and how much I wanted to kiss her. My heart was racing and my palms were sweaty and all I wanted was to kiss her and hold her in my arms. We are here… I am here at the base of the cave system.

Welcome to level one, says the voice in my head.

"It seems quiet here on the first level," says Renée as we walk on the dirty and dusty floor.

We are not alone. I can sense them, but cannot see them. I know we are walking into a trap.

She knows I have come. Fuck it, if this is a trap… Let's see what they have got. I am prepared to bleed every one of those vampires dry until I kill her. Wait a minute…

I shoot a glance at Alex and he looks back at me. He senses exactly what I do. Millions of bloodsuckers lurking around us; some smell more than several millennia old. They may be around us, but they reek of fear. They should be. This is their final night on this Earth. I hope she remembers this moment well into the afterlife. The one person she messed with will be the end of her entire species. They are moving fast, so fast that they flood the empty cave within seconds. We are surrounded.

"Here they are," says Alex as he moves closer to us.

The horde of vampires charges us from the shadows all at once. This is going to be a massacre. I will relish their blood.

Alex lets out a primal scream that echoes through the cave as he transforms into the werewolf. Bullets ricochet around the room as we battle our way through the constant onslaught of vampires. They keep coming one by one.

"Alex!" I yell to him as a signal to let out his army.

The werewolf's primal howl echoes throughout room. The sound reverberates through the cave system. More vampires continue to rush in. Our goal is to get to the levels below. This mission seems harder than anticipated. Vampires and humans begin to lose people to this fight.

* * *

I watch Ajay rip through those vampires one by one. He is intense and fuelled solely by the purpose of removing what he calls a curse. I… I… Let's just hold that thought for a while; multiple vampires surround me. They charge towards me. I raise my hands and summon the power of the air around us. I wish I understood these powers; it's as if I can talk to the air with my mind. A group of vampires jump up into the air, trying to pounce on me, but I use the air around them to slam them into the ground, crushing them to death. Their bodies splatter like bugs on a concrete floor; blood and parts of their anatomy are scattered all over the room. Right… where was I? Uh… Yes, I was watching Ajay. I see the change in him and this is so much darker than the glimpses that I witnessed. Seeing him cold-heartedly draining the blood of those vampires… My breathing increases as I recall that night. The look on Ajay's face was different. He felt some remorse then; I know, because I saw it in his eyes, but that remorse and those emotions are no longer there. He is still mine, my Ajay, and I will do whatever it takes for him to realise that, no matter what, I will always love him. I still just watch him with all that hatred he has. All I want to say to him is 'just let it go', but I also now understand his pain. I understand his desire to be the old Ajay and all of this was because of me.

* * *

"*Alex!*" I yell as the horde of vampires continues to grow.

Ria is on the other end carving a path towards me. Alex is busy tearing through a few vampires of his own.

After that horrifying howl from Alex, the ground begins to rumble as if there is a stampede on its way towards us. The sand below us and the pebbles around the room vibrate. The ceiling caves in as Andrew drills his way through the ground above using his wings. He continues to drill through the ground we are on and continues through to levels below as he heads deep into the hive. The hordes of vampires are unfazed by the distractions. They continue to fill the room. A never-ending and exhausting horde follows.

"Alex, where are they?" asks Renée.

Hooowwwllll.

The sounds of wolves howling can be heard in the distance. I hear them, but where are they from?

Hooowwwlllll.

The sounds are coming from above. The howls are faint, but are growing louder with every passing second. I try to scan above. I can see something, but am not sure what I am seeing. A figure appears from above in the tunnel created by Andrew. It is dusty in the cave, but some light comes in from above. The shadowy figure seems to have the head of a wolf and the body of a man.

This creature turns to the hordes and bellows out a deathly howl. The dust intensifies as a few dozen more of these creatures stand behind the first. Alex howls back; he must know them. An echo of howls are heard through the cave; this rattles the horde of vampires. They pause. We all do.

The wolf-like people lunge forward, attacking the vampires with an aggressive force, tearing them apart one by one. I look at the creatures and then at Alex.

"What the hell are those things?" I ask Alex.

"Well, I call them zombie werewolves; it's a side effect from my bite," replies Alex.

"Zombie werewolves? Yep, that makes total sense," I say as I move to the huge hole in the ground, thanks to Andrew.

Zombie fucking werewolves; yep, mindless killing machines designed to kill vampires. This day cannot get any weirder. I feel heated, as if my blood is being boiled. The guardians are coming; that is what I feel. I can feel my skin burn. The pain… pain… I am on the floor on my knees. The pain… I am trying, but I cannot express the pain. I roll over and fall through the hole.

* * *

The guardians burst through the cave floor. There are hundreds of thousands of guardians and they join the fight. Renée and her team are brave, even in the face of these monsters. The zombie werewolves turn their attention to the guardians. They do not fear these monsters as they slash their way through the creatures. They are doing more than just hurting the guardians. The body of a guardian falls to the dirt. The thud of its lifeless body makes a noise that is louder than any echo that vibrates the cave. Everyone stops to look at the death of the guardian, caused by a single zombie.

I look around. I see Alex, Renée, the soldiers and Alex's army, but no Ajay.

"Alex, where is Ajay?" I yell.

"He was near the hole before those things popped up," says Alex as he continues tearing apart a guardian. He is the perfect hunter.

Those things – he meant guardians. No. No. No. I have to find him. I rush towards the hole in the ground.

"*Ajay!*" I yell as I jump in.

I try to feel his presence, scanning every level as I reach the lower level. I sense him, but it is so dark down here. A beam of light showers the area around me. I step out of the light and into the darkness, in search of light in the darkness. I can feel his presence much stronger now. My eyes are readjusting to the darkness and I can now see a group of guardians surrounding a body in the distance. I can hear grunting and now a scream.

Aaaaaarrrrgggghhhh!

They are hurting my Ajay. I raise my hand and clench my hand. All I can think right now is that I have to save him. The air around the guardians begins to shift violently as I throw two of the guardians across the room. I use a vortex of wind to shelter him as I rush over to shield him with my body.

"It's okay," says Ajay.

I see another guardian flying towards us and I stand up to take it on when I hear another echo. I turn to Ajay and see him biting a huge chunk out of the guardian. Ajay has transformed into the monstrous creature. He stares into a space far into the distance.

What are you looking at, Ajay? What is out there? Can it be he has finally found the vampire for whom he has been searching?

Screeeeeeeeeeeeeeeeeeeeeccccchhhhhh!

A scream echoes in the distance. Beast Ajay has vanished, but, in the corner of the dark room, I see Andrew. There is blood around him and he is unconscious. I go closer to him to check up on him. Where has Ajay gone?

I hear another echoing scream rumble through the room. The scream is getting louder; the sound is unbearable. I cannot stand. I fall to the floor. I try to shift the air around us to create a barrier, but the echo of the scream is stronger. I try to push the air to the side so I can grab Andrew and take him to safety. The figure of a woman can be seen in the distance. She screams and the sound vibrates the room and returns to itself, creating a larger echo like a tsunami of waves crashing into each other, over and over, becoming more powerful. A large hand with long fingers ending in longer fingernails grabs the woman's neck from behind and brings her into the light.

* * *

"Alina," I say as I look into her eyes.

She does not recognise me. Her eyes are ravenous for the blood of her victims. She takes a deep breath and screams at me. I immediately release my grip and hurtle back several feet. I have to get back to her. I have to make her understand who she is.

"*Ria!*" I yell as she and Andrew, who has now revived from his incident, rush over to me.

"Vortex," I utter to Ria, watching her look at me in amazement that I am able to control this version of myself.

Ria looks at Alina and then begins to wave at the air and create a vortex. I rise and look at Ria.

"I know her, but she doesn't remember me," I say to Ria.

"I may have a way. Place your…" says Ria as she stares at my claws. "…Hand on my shoulder."

I can barely hear her; my ears are still ringing. The ringing is so loud. I keep trying to reach for a phone that is not there. Haha. At least my humour is still intact, but is that blood rolling down my neck? Whatever she is, she is definitely powerful. She won't kill me, but she will probably hurt me a lot. I place my 'hands' on Ria's shoulder and, in the blink of an eye, I am transported into a bunker. I know this place. I have been here before, many times before. This room has a control panel and a two-way mirror. Wait a second… Is that me?

"Hey!" says a voice I have not heard in a long time.

"Alina," I reply as I turn to the door.

She is standing there as if she is about to enter the room.

She stares at me and then at the other me through the two-way mirror.

"Two of you?" She gasps at the sight.

"Forget him," I say as I look at the other me.

I notice her reaching for her weapon. Slight distrust there.

Bang!

She shot me. What the fuck is wrong with her? She shot me. I pick the smashed bullet from my shirt and flick it to the floor.

"Funny, you should know better than that," I say to her angrily.

She still has that weapon trained on me. She has an intense 'I am gonna fuck you up' look.

"Do you know where you are?" I ask her.

"Do you, arsehole?" she retorts in an aggressive tone.

"I do, but do you really know where you are?" I reply as she quickly surveys the room.

"In the basement of the bunker. Why are you asking such a dumb question?" asks Alina.

"What year is it?" I enquire, only as a gauge to see her reaction.

"Year? Seriously!" she snarls at me.

"Yes, year. What year is it, Alina?" I ask.

Her demeanour changes to one of concern. I can see it in her eyes. She is trying to make sense of the fact that there are two of me and even more so that I am making weird enquiries.

"It's 1991," she replies, still staring a hole through me.

"That was forty-seven years ago. Truly look at me and tell me if I am the same as… as him," I say as I look at my old self.

Alina stares at me for a few seconds and then looks around the room. She is struggling with the thought of having lost more than forty years of her life.

"What is the last thing you remember before you got to this room?" I ask.

She looks back at me and then at fake me. "I was talking to Renée about this mansion with a bell tower," she says, desperately trying to recall her last moment.

"The last time I saw you was on the staircase under the mansion with the bell tower. The staircase exploded and then you were gone, but that was not the last time I remember of you. The last time I remember of you was when you said 'you can trust Renée', but the words that echoed that night were 'let go of the hate'. I wish I took your advice on both," I say.

The ceiling begins to vibrate and break up. Pieces of the ceiling fall to the floor as it breaks away and vanishes. The room begins to unravel and explode into nothingness. This world is vanishing around us, the table, chairs, equipment and even the floor. There we stand, Alina, me and fake me.

She just looks at me and then at fake me as it explodes into the abyss.

"What now?" she asks.

I wish I knew. How do we get out?

Something is here. I can sense it; it is nearby. Over there… I turn and there stands another Alina. This one is much darker and scarier. It seems like the feral monster in the cave. A banshee.

"You have to fight your way out. This battle is your and yours alone," I say to her as I am pushed out of this world.

* * *

The ringing in my ear is back. I am back in the cave. Ria is beside me. I am no longer the monster. I am trying to focus back into this world. I turn to her as a droplet of my blood falls onto Ria's hand with a burning reaction that sends her back into the wall wailing in pain.

"What the hell?" she yells.

I wipe the blood from my neck.

"It was just blood," I say to her as I try to piece together how this is possible.

"That is not possible," Ria replies.

Alina begins to move. Ria and I move slightly closer to one another as we prepare to fight banshee Alina one more time.

The banshee stumbles to her feet, searching the room. Ria moves a step forward. The banshee looks at us. Ria moves a step forward again and is preparing to attack.

"Ajay!" Alina calls to me in desperation.

I walk towards her. "Hey, A, you good?" I ask her as I inch closer.

"I could be better," she replies.

Ria and I go to her side, but I sense something. I know this presence. I felt this once before. I see a silhouette of it in the distance. I turn to the darkest corner of the room. You are there, aren't you? I can feel every part of me scream at her. Forty-seven years, I have waited for this moment. I step forward and, as I do, I immediately transform into the eight-foot monster. There is no violent change; it is instinctive. I see you.

"I remember you," I say to the monster before me.

She has changed too. She is slightly larger than I am.

"This curse ends tonight," I say to the monster.

It does not speak; it just stares at me.

"You are just going to stand there and say nothing. You stole my whole world from me and you just stand there and *say nothing! You fucking monster, you stole everything from me!*" I yell as loudly as I can at this villainous monster.

It makes no difference to her.

I lunge forward and wrap my claws around her neck. I sink my teeth into her neck, tearing a huge part from her neck as I pull away. She just stands there. She is motionless. Those bright yellowish eyes continue to just stare at me. The blood in her body begins to break down and disintegrate. The skin peels from the monster and bleeds from her bones like honey dripping off a tree. I don't care about the death of this monster, but I question how much of a monster I have become that the only thing I can think about is myself. There it is. I still see the claws. I still remain the same. All of that, all of the time, all of the lives and all of that effort to end this fucking curse and all of it was *bullshit!*

I will never be human.

There is no changing back. I am stuck as this immortal being. Killing her was supposed to make this all better; why do I not feel any better? I feel lost.

"Satisfied?" asks a deep voice from deeper in the cave. "Now can you leave my people alone."

I turn to him. He is slightly larger than she is. How is it possible? Why is it possible? I did not sense this monster.

How can there be another? The aura around him is different; it is hiding something.

Screeeeeeeeeech!

A loud bellow is directed at the monster. The room is vibrating like an earthquake trembling the ground around us. The deafening scream echoes through the room with destructive force, but the monster still stands, unfazed by Alina. I can see her behind the monster. She is giving it all she has. He turns to her and, with a single motion of his claws, the sound of the scream stops and she is now trying to cough.

"Insolent child!" he says as she is choking, and then she is flung across the room towards me.

The monster turns back to me and just looks at me with a 'please get these beings out of my space' expression. I rush over to Alina as I transform back into my human self. He watches me in awe.

"How are you able to change so easily?" asks the monster.

At this moment, it does not hit me, as my focus remains on Alina and this damn monster in front of me. Why is me transforming so odd to him?

"Does it matter? How are you possible?" I ask him, still trying to figure out how this monster is here.

"There is more of me than you could ever imagine," he replies. "Your transformation matters, young one." He looks at his claws and back at me. "If only… If only I could see…" he says as he caresses his face with his claws. "But that time is long gone. Seeing you now makes me think that maybe it is possible."

Ria races over to Alina and me.

"One more?" she asks.

I nod at her and turn my attention back to the monster.

"Take your people and leave me and my kind alone," says the monster.

I notice Alex and Andrew in the distance. I think he does too. Do we just leave? We should.

You definitely should, says the voice in my head.

You are right, voice in my head. We should. We should walk away… but I want to kill him. He may have this hidden thing about him, but I smell vampire in there. I am trying to hold back, but fuck it. I lunge forward as fast as I can. Midway through my stride, I transform back into the monster. I raise my hands to slash at him, but he vanishes and reappears in front of Andrew. He grabs Andrew by his wings and throws him hard into the wall somewhere in the darkness.

"I take this as a sign of war," he says.

"Take it however you want. You will all die," says Alex as he jumps towards the monster, but he is swatted away like he is nothing.

I look at Ria as she is about to prepare to attack the monster.

"Stay back," I say to her.

She looks at me with a bit of that old defiant nature. I rush him again, but he once again vanishes and instantly appears behind me. He grabs me with his massive claws that cover my head. It is hard to breathe. He is suffocating me, but I know now that, no matter what happens, I will not die. He lifts me into the air. Helpless; that is what I am feeling right now. He is overpowering me. I am clawing at his hands and his face and body. Funny, a moment ago, I was confident of my immortality. If he does not kill me, this is still going to hurt like I am almost at death's door. Now I know what those vampires felt before I ripped them apart. He is trying and I can feel my body being stretched apart. The atoms are being pulled apart, but they are also fighting to stay together.

Booooom!

A sonic blast sends shockwaves that hit us full-on. His grip on me remains tight; he seems unfazed. The attack gives Andrew and Alex enough time to launch an attack of their own. I can hear the sounds of claws scrapping on hardened flesh. Their attack is quick and relentless as they flash past us at an increasing pace.

Whooosh.

Whooosh.

Whooosh.

Andrew slashes at the monster with his wings.

"*Aaaarrrrgghhh!*" the monster yells as he flings me into Alex and Andrew, hurtling us across the room.

My body crashes into the cave wall, leaving an indentation in it. I have been imprinted into the core of this world.

I crawl to Alex. My breathing is much faster.

"I know what I am about to ask you is going to sound idiotic, but I have done the math. He is stronger and faster than all of us and, by my count, we are going to be dead. There is more inside him; I can feel it, but I'm still unable to understand why I cannot see it," I say to Alex.

"What are you asking?" asks Alex.

Without hesitation, I look at Alex and say, "I need you to bite me."

"*What!*" he exclaims, clearly thinking I am insane.

"I think I can use what is inside you to become as strong as that thing," I say to him as Alina and Ria fight the monster.

It is able to grab Ria and throw her across the room. She looks winded.

"*Merde!* Are you fucking nuts? Look at that thing. Even if you could, what do you think would happen to you if I bite you? Don't forget the army of mindless controlled zombies up there. If I bite you, you could become one of those things," he says as he turns to the monster and then back to me.

"We cannot destroy that monster just like this. As much as this is the dumbest idea I have ever had, this is our best shot," I say as I watch the monster bite Ria's neck and then throw her to the floor. "Alex, he is stronger and faster than all of us," I say as Ria stands up again.

Alex looks at the monster and then grabs my arm.

"This is seriously a bad fucking idea," says Alex as he bites my arm. "Now what?"

"Stall him," I say as I feel the plasma from the bite run through my veins.

Alex gets up and rushes to Andrew in the darkness.

"*Your attempts are futile!*" yells the monster.

Ria creates a vortex around the monster, draining the air around it, but, once again, it seems futile, as he said. He is able to breathe in the vortex. Andrew flies around the vortex at a super pace. The monster shatters the vortex. Andrew uses his wings as swords and begins to slice the monster's body and face repeatedly. Alex jumps onto the monster, using his claws on the beast. After a series of attacks, he just stands there. The wounds begin to heal themselves. The monster bellows an echoing scream; it sounds like Alina. The room violently vibrates and a wave of sound blasts the trio into the walls again.

"Now, you die," he says with confidence. "Now, you all die, insolent filth. Your kinds are beneath a god of my stature."

Hope is lost. Death… real death is among us. They know they are outmatched. There is one last attack before…

Hoooooooowwwwwwwwllllllll!

Alex looks at the hole in the ceiling.

"That's not one of my zombies," says Alex.

They all look towards this new creature. It stands more than ten feet tall and has a mix of werewolf features and large wings. The creature vanishes. The monster stands there and looks at his chest. There are claw marks and blood flowing from the wounds. The monster is not healing as fast as before. A second and third strike of claw marks land on the monster's face and back. It still heals from them. This monster will not die, but maybe I can wound him enough for her. I claw him several times before I hold him as tightly as I can. He is a massive monster, more than nine feet tall, with massive wings too. I scan the room. This new body has abilities much greater than before. I know I am still not able to kill this fucking monster, but I can see this fucker now. He cannot hide from me. I smell all the strains whirling their way through his system. The being is ancient. Alina and Andrew are further down the hall and are still hurt. This wolf blood is powerful. I can feel my strength growing each passing moment. I am stronger and mixed with the power of the divine force and perfect hunter. He is fighting me, but I manage to hold on to him. I am still scanning the room. Oh… Oh, that's right; there you are.

"*Ria!*" I yell.

She looks at me and then, in an instant, she propels herself with great force into this vile being. I can feel his body twitching. I release him. I now can see. I see…

"*Half-breed, what have you done to me?*" yells the high vampire.

"Death calls to you. Do you hear it?" I ask him as I watch his body violently tremble.

He stares a hole through my soul. I can see her as she yells before blood and matter splatter throughout the cave.

He is dead. The immortal being is dead. There she is. There is my Ria, still like always. She stands there majestic and perfect in every way. Here I stand, still a monster, even further away from my humanity than I ever was and with no hope of returning to the Ajay of 1990. I finally realise that those days are far gone and I will live like this forever. My life will be one of continuous pain and suffering coupled with the lust for blood until the end of this planet. That is not the worst part of all this. I will have to be away from Ria. I understand now why she was hurt by my blood. It is the poisoned divine blood that is in my system. This version of me is poison to her and now I cannot shed this form either. I am stuck as this were-vamp hybrid. I have lost. I have lost myself in the pursuit of my humanity and I have lost her, twice now. I look at Alina, Andrew and Alex. There is a smell to them. I can smell them and it smells so good. The hunger has returned and, as much as I am trying to fight… It is so strong, stronger than before, and I can only see the blood coursing through their veins…

No, Ajay! You cannot…

I thought this road would lead to the end of my misery, but now I understand that I am no better than those monsters. I can hear the beings above scurrying away. The hunger is getting stronger.

"You have to be the one," I say to Ria as she turns to me and looks at the hideous monster I have become. "You were always the one to take the hard road for both of us.

You need to be stronger now. I say this, but we both know that you have always been strong. I wish I was one tenth as strong as you are, but I never was. What I am going to ask…" I say as I feel the tears roll down my face. I can see the teardrops falling from her face as well. I wipe away my tears. "You have to kill me."

* * *

Those words echoed through my soul, vibrating through every fibre of my being as Ajay says them. I stand there emotionless. I am too stunned to move. All I can think about is every moment we shared and every moment we could have made. I love him too much. I love him too much to…

How do I?

* * *

I can see the struggle she is going through.

How could she kill me?

I know what I asked of her and I can see the struggle she has with it, but I have no choice.

* * *

"There must be another way," I say to Ajay in the hopes that he has another plan. This cannot be the only way.

* * *

She is still struggling with this, but this monster I have created is no better than those monsters we killed.

* * *

I walk closer to Ajay. I can feel the stream of tears on my face. I try to caresses his face. I place my hand on his skin and it feels cold at first, but my hand begins to light up and glow. My hand is on fire. I pull back my hand as fast I can. There are scorch marks on my hand.

"*What the hell?*" I yell as I stare at Alina and Alex, and then I turn back to Ajay.

* * *

She stares at Alina and Alex and then turns back to me. I can see the fear in her eyes, but I can see she understands now.

"I love you," she utters, and then she vanishes.

"I love you forever," I say as I feel a gust of wind blow into my body.

I take one last look at my friends, Alina, Alex and Andrew. I look at the cave walls and, in an instant, I light up in a blinding white light.

* * *

The porch… I am on this fucking porch again. I am back here again, after everything. I am right back here. I go to the door and open it to go back into the house and there she stands as I enter. There is Ahana once again on top of those stairs looking at me.

"Mum," she says.

"Not again. Why am I back here?" I ask her.

She just stares at me.

Ding-dong.

The doorbell rings.

"Why here?" I ask Ahana as I turn to open the door.

"This is the point that it all started," says Ahana.

I open the door as I have done many times before. The door opens and there is a bright flash of light and a series of flashes of light, and everything goes dark.

* * *

I open my eyes. The light hurts a bit. I try to focus and I see a face. It is weird; I don't recognise this… I am lying on a bed and she is next to me. She has snow-white hair and her skin is a bit shrivelled; she looks like she is in her 80s. I know her, but I am not sure… There is something about her energy and her vibe; that's my Ria. I see it. I see it in her smile. This is my dream. She is awake.

"Ajay," she says.

"Yes, Ria," I reply.

"Where are we?" she asks as she looks around.

We are in a bedroom. The room is decorated in purple and there is a smell of lavender in the air.

"Whenever I looked at you, I always pictured this moment. You and me. Us in our 80s lying in a bed together staring at each other. I would lose myself in your eyes. I wake up and look at you and wonder… How lucky I am that I get to wake up next to the most perfect person in the world and I remember that I love you more each day we have been together. This was what I pictured our perfect future would be. You and me, here in this moment," I say to Ria.

"What do we do now?" she asks.

"Nothing; that's the beauty of this. We don't have to be anywhere but here. There is nowhere I would rather be than right here next to you," I say to Ria.

"Sounds perfect," Ria says to me.

CHAPTER NINE

Epilogue

"They just left us here," says Alex.

The darkness engulfs the cave once again, masking the death and despair that came before it. You can smell it in the air, the decay of blood and plasma that surrounds us. Alina grabs Andrew and turns to Alex. The howls of the zombies come from above.

"Ajay's path was always going to end in death," says Andrew. "He was reborn out of death, his decisions led him to more death, and his end had to be in death."

Alex looks at Andrew and then at Alina. "He fucking speaks."

She just smiles at Alex.

Alex looks back at Andrew and says, "I get that, but did you not hear that monster? There are more of them out there. It took all of us to hurt this one and it then took two super-beings to finally kill it. What do you think is going to happen when we come across another of these?"

Alina turns back to Alex as she carries Andrew to the hole in the ceiling.

"Do you think that matters at this point? It took us more than fifty years to find these things and none of us knew about them," says Alina.

"We just killed two of their own," says Alex as he jumps up into the ceiling.

"They did just leave us," says Alina as she stares at the sunlight seeping through the hole from above.

This is the first time Alina has been in contact with light in more than twenty years. Her future and the fate of the world now lay in the hands of a werewolf, birdman and her – a banshee.

Hoooooowwwwwwwllllll!

The final howls of the zombie werewolves – yes, it still is the dumbest thing – can be heard from the levels above.